SUBMIT

A NOVEL

NATASHA LEWIN

Library of Congress Control Number: 2026906773
Paperback ISBN: 979-8-9953003-0-4
Hardcover ISBN: 979-8-9953003-1-1
eBook ISBN: 979-8-9953003-2-8

Published by Stage of Grace Press, Los Angeles, CA

Cover design by Steve Kuhn

Human Authored Reg. #8991366

✝ HUMAN AUTHORED

For my husband

1

SMACK!

Dee's right cheek kissed the pavement as she tumbled to the ground.

"Not again," she groaned.

She lay on her belly. Arms splayed, palms covered with gravel, and the burn of a skinned knee. She ran through her how-bad-is-it checklist: Forehead. Nose. No red wetness. Her right cheekbone stung. A bruise already blooming. She blinked, tested her vision. No blur.

"I'm okay," she said. "Thankfully." Her attempts at praise were as clumsy as her body. Before she could brush herself off, the familiar huffing of another runner closed in.

Beep beep beep.

The Garmin on her wrist blared. Dee froze, willing herself invisible. As the runner entered her periphery, she planted her right leg in a mock calf stretch. Her left knee buckled, reopening the abrasion. She held her breath. The runner passed by without greeting. Once the sound drifted into the distance, Dee exhaled.

Peace lasted three seconds, then advice from her gynecologist invaded her mind.

Try foreplay.

Guilt flooded through Dee like ice water. She broke down and sobbed into her bloodied, pebble-flecked hands.

She tried to focus on her run. Her earbuds were feeding her a self-help audiobook. They failed her too. All she could hear was Dr. Bruder's flippant diagnosis. Hormonal changes. Thinning tissue. Impossible sex. A libido on life support. No amount of "foreplay" could undo going into early menopause at the age of thirty-eight. Because of it, she and Eric only consummated their marriage once in six months. And it wasn't even on their wedding night.

Dee's masochistic mind drifted to scripture — a default drilled into her since youth.

Wives, submit yourselves to your own husbands as you do to the Lord.

"What a joke," she said, scoffing at Ephesians 5:22.

Dr. Bruder plus childhood memories multiplied by wife-shaming scripture equaled stress. The verse gnawed at her as she propelled herself down the bike path in a hobble. Trees and bushes blurred. Shame nipped at her ankles.

I can't have sex. My body's broken. Maybe Eric and I should get a divorce.

2

Greenup, Kentucky was smaller than Peoria. A population of less than 1,500 compared to Peoria's 100,000-plus. Greenup sat at the confluence of two rivers, the Little Sandy and the Ohio, while Peoria grew up along the mighty Illinois. Greenup offered mostly outdoorsy options: parks, covered bridges, lakes, and the two rivers. While Greenup was most definitely not Peoria, it shared enough commonalities (and differences) for Dee to feel close enough to home.

In the early 2000s, when Dee was twenty-one, she purchased her three-bedroom house for $68,000, cash. The expansive back-yard butted up against the Little Sandy and included its own dock and dinghy. Apple, pear, peach, and plum trees blanketed the four-acre parcel. A recent addition of a three-seasons room increased both the home's charm and its equity. No pictures of her family hung on the walls, but memories of them lived everywhere.

In one of her two-and-a-half bathrooms, Dee washed blood and grit from her hands and face. The bump on her cheek flared with tenderness at her touch.

How am I going to explain this one?

Dee studied the bruise as it shifted from red to purple. An old yellowing bruise on her hip and a week-old scratch on her knee winked at her.

This is why I'm losing customers. Who wants advice from a clumsy runner?

Dee couldn't focus on the good. Like owning her own home. Running her own business. Or even Eric, her loving, patient husband who never pressured her about their lack of intimacy.

Despite the bumps and bruises, none of Dee's recent falls injured her too badly. Her body and head remained strong. Her spirit did not.

Though much in her life deserved gratitude, Dee clung only to the negative. She wanted to travel back in time and stay there.

She turned on the shower, where she could go completely passive. Like she was floating inside her mother's womb. Her body craved intimacy as much as she shunned it. She tucked her dark curls into her shower cap and stepped into the heat. Filtered water splashed against her ebony skin. Dee lathered her torso. Fingers worked tight muscles loose. The shower's gentle caress warmed her body where the run had chilled it. Her fingers drifted south. Gooseflesh rippled across her ribs and taut stomach. She gently washed her womanhood, a place that ached with solitude. A place that ached, period.

Dee growled at the intrusion of menopause and the reminder of her duty to have sex.

This shower is the wettest I'll ever be.

3

Dee pulled mental panties over her naked vulnerability. She shut off the water with a sigh. Plush towel draped around her sore body, she padded into her closet to dress for the day.

The walk-in was the size of a New York City studio apartment and just as expensive. She had burned through more than half of her eight-million-dollar inheritance in less than ten years. Racks upon racks of organized frocks hung on hangers like dead meat. She tried donating the bounty, but the women's shelter in Lexington refused name brands for safety reasons.

Dee chose a sleeveless white blouse and a pair of stretchy jeans from the Target in West Virginia. It was the closest to Greenup and still an hour away. Her fingers fastened the cheap buttons. She'd worn this same shirt almost six years earlier after finishing the International Half Marathon. The race marked her first trip to Canada. Over the years, Dee traveled often. Mostly for races. Sometimes to escape around Mother's Day and Father's Day. When her family was alive, Dee was always homesick when away from them. Now she was always away from them.

The first mile Dee ever ran filled her with more purpose than any shopping spree or scripture ever did. But when she returned home, she was hollowed out and lonely. She chased that same mix of anticipation and depletion day after day. Opening Run Café was the same as a drunk opening a bar. The business was built for a patron of one.

In Kentucky, she grew close to no one. Not even her sole employee. She kept her life private and settled into a friendless rhythm. Dee judged too harshly. Trust didn't come easily. She'd been let down before, hard.

Most notably by God.

4

———

Solomon's smelled sharp and chemical. Twelve-year-old Dee stood on a step stool stocking jars of relaxer onto newly mounted shelves. Even sealed, the stuff announced itself. It made the fine hairs at the nape of her neck prickle, as if her own head were next.

Late-afternoon light poured in through wide windows, warming the honey-colored wood floors Morris had finished just days before. Outside, November weather pressed closer. Leaves skittered across sidewalks. The sun hung too bright and too warm for the late Peoria fall.

Dee reached in the box and lifted another jar. Her hands sweaty, the jar slipped. Glass shattered. Shards glittered across the floor, catching sunlight like tiny, sharp knives.

"You okay, DeeDee?" Morris asked. He took out a broom and started to sweep.

"Yes, sir."

He smiled and handed the broom to her. "Finish up for me then."

She bent and swept, careful. The smell of relaxer thickened. Her burning eyes blinked and looked away. Shifting shadows moved across the hardwood as the sun lowered. Outside, a pointed black hat streaked past the window. Her sister Rashida pressed her nose to the glass.

"They're coming," she said. Rashida was eight, already restless. "Mama, look."

"I see them," Mavis said. She adjusted a shelf of hair oils near the register, labels turned just so. "Y'all remember what tonight is?"

"Not a night for us," Rashida recited. Her eyes glued to the street. Children in costume moved in clusters. Their plastic pumpkins bobbing with candy.

Dee swept slower. She wanted to go every year but she had learned not to ask. A knock came at the door. She looked up at a little girl with green skin, a drawn-on wart, and natural box braids. Her patterned pillowcase heavy and low.

"No," Dee mouthed. Her pointer finger waggled. Before the witch could disappear—

"Wait," Mavis said. "Open that."

Morris crossed the room and unlocked the door. The little girl stepped in. Eyes wide. She held out her bag.

"Trick or treat."

Mavis reached in her purse, pulled out a five-dollar bill, and dropped it in the pillowcase.

"Treat," she said.

The witch looked in her bag, Black-green face falling.

"No candy?"

Mavis smiled. "Money buys candy too."

Dee punctuated her mother's words with a nod. She knew money was better.

The witch hesitated. Shrugged. Ran back outside and waved the bill. "They're only giving money," she shouted to the others.

Children booed. Morris and Mavis laughed.

Why'd Mom do that if Halloween is so bad?

Mavis turned back to the register. "Let's head out. The sun's going down."

Chapter 4

Morris looped an arm around Rashida's shoulders. "Come on, pumpkin."

The smell of relaxer wrapped around Dee, stinky yet comforting. She breathed through her mouth and kept her eyes on the floor. Only one tiny shard of glass remained. She noticed how the light made the most dangerous things beautiful.

5

Dee lay on her narrow bed, electric blanket pulled to her chin. Heat hummed beneath her. Heavy snow stacked on the windowsill. The radiator knocked and hissed. Heather hadn't made it back from winter break yet. It was just Dee in her dorm room, all alone.

She held Kelly Brown Douglas's *The Black Christ* open, its spine bent and cracked under her thumbs. Dee tried to read her homework, but the words all slid past her. She flipped the page.

"Christianity and Cruelty."

She flipped the page back, distracted.

They should be home by now.

A burst of noise broke through the stillness. Voices echoed down the hall. Dee lifted her head at the interruption. Suddenly, a knock at her door.

"Dee?"

Dee frowned. She brought her feet onto the floor. The carpet was cold beneath the thin soles of her fuzzy pink bunny slippers. Rashida's gift from Christmas. Dee didn't take them off all day. Anything to remind her of home.

Her RA, Amanda, stood at the door. Head freshly buzzed.

Chapter 5

Red-and-black flannel. Silver hoop in her nose. Tears mixed with the splash of freckles spotting her face.

"There's been an accident." Dee waited for the rest. Amanda held out a slip of paper. Her hand shook. "Call this."

Dee took the paper. A number she didn't recognize printed in black ink.

"Why?"

Amanda sniffled. "Your parents and sister—" Dee's eyebrows locked together. Amanda's voice cracked. "They were in an accident."

The hallway tilted. Red-and-black flannel swirled. "Are they okay?"

Amanda's gaze dropped. A drop of snot blew from her nose to the ground.

"No."

Something about police. Black ice. A truck. The words arrived muffled. Dee's knees softened. The world folded in on itself. She fell to the ground.

6

Dean O'Connor's office smelled like stale smoke and lemony Pledge. Dee sat in a soft leather chair that drooped sadly in the middle. When she shifted, it creaked and moaned like her chattering teeth. The chair faced a dark-mahogany desk. Behind it, matching shelves climbed toward an expansive ceiling. A place built to make people feel small.

Books lined the shelves, spines clean and uncracked. Framed photographs sat everywhere. Dee's eyes drifted to each picture. The U of I football team. A ribbon cutting. O'Connor shaking hands with a man in a suit. She counted the Black faces. One. Barack Obama.

Dee's electric blanket sat around her shoulders unplugged. Her snow boots were bulky and damp. Same with her feet. She forgot socks. Frost clung to her soles, seeping through her bones. A chill ran through her. She was just as frozen as the people behind the glassy frames on the shelves.

Dean O'Connor sat across from her like the therapist from *The Sopranos.* Not that Dee ever watched it. She was never allowed. The smoking pipe on his desk sat beside an unused ink blotter that was more for show.

She concentrated on his hands. How he folded them. Clasped

them. Opened them wide. Like he was kneading invisible dough. Dee wondered what it must be like to be Deaf and be able to read motion instead of listening to words. She wished she had that gift now.

"I'm so sorry, Dionne," he said more than once.

He used her full name. It landed on her skin like a mosquito. No one called her Dionne unless she was in trouble. She did not correct him. She did not offer Dee. She did not offer him anything. She could not open her mouth.

On O'Connor's desk sat tissues inside an embroidered tissue box. The native design did not fit the Irish dean's office aesthetic. He slid the box toward her with one finger. She stared at it as if she could make it explode.

Dee rubbed at the cuticle on her thumb and picked the dry skin open until it bled on purpose. Her childhood dentist said that the human body could not feel two points of pain at the same time. She was testing his theory with her heart and her hand.

"Here," O'Connor said, holding out the tissue box. "You're bleeding."

Dee took one because it seemed easier than refusing. The Kleenex was heavy and expensive, like the rest of the room. She pressed it to her nose and blew. O'Connor's eyebrows shot from above his horn rims and into the sky. When they settled back to his face, he spoke.

"You don't need to make any decisions right now," he said, as if he had practiced the line. "You don't need to think about class. We can put everything on hold."

Dee bore down on her jaw so hard her gums hurt.

"We have resources and people you can talk to. We can help you get home."

Home.

The word made her stomach twist. It made her want to flip his desk. It made her want to throw up again. Only this time, her puke would be all over O'Connor instead of her R.A.

Dee lifted her eyes to the photographs again. A woman in

pearls. A man in a military uniform. A kid playing soccer. Dee imagined each of them walking in and out of this office with their families intact.

O'Connor cleared his throat. "Do you have anyone you can call? Or that we can?" he added, remembering his oath as a dean.

Dee's lips parted slightly. Once, she had three people. They had always been four.

Now only one.

She zippered her mouth shut. O'Connor waited. The silence stretched. He tried again. "Aunts? Uncles? Grandparents?"

Dee looked at him then. His eyes held pity, but something else floated under it.

Fear.

Dee's tight jaw unhinged with a squeak. "No." She cleared her throat, unsure about the last time she'd had a conversation. Or if she'd ever be able to hold one again.

"Okay," he said softly. He glanced toward a notepad on his desk. "I knew your parents, Mavis and Morris." He said their names slowly and carefully. Like a person who used to have a stutter. "My office worked with them for years." He put his shoulders back proudly. "They supported our students of color in meaningful ways. Long before you ever applied."

Dee's thumb throbbed. A drop of blood fell on her blanket.

He went on, voice smoothing out with confidence. "They believed in this institution. They cared deeply about education. They cared about you."

Dee stared past him. Past the wood. Past the walls. As if she could see through the building and out into the storm.

Dean O'Connor exhaled his patience. "One thing I know about Mavis and Morris Moreland, they would want you to keep going."

Dee's eyes grew hot. Her thumb throbbed. Pain in more than two spots.

My dentist is a liar.

"You have no idea what they'd want." Her words came out with a serrated edge.

O'Connor blinked. He backpedaled. He was one step away from a microaggression against a student in mourning.

"Of course," he said. "My apologies."

His hands folded and unfolded again. Dee watched his fingers and read them.

He's afraid of the mess.

O'Connor continued. "Your father," he chose his words carefully, "was a big man."

"My dad was the same height as me."

She cracked her knuckles. The fight was on.

O'Connor's face distorted. "Big in heart is what I meant." He recalibrated. "He was big in generosity."

Was.

The past tense punched Dee harder than any of the dean's other words. O'Connor reached toward the tissue box again, then stopped himself. "Your family." He said their names again. "Mavis and Morris."

Dee waited for him to say Rashida, but he didn't. She was supposed to be starting at Purdue in the fall.

She stared at the snotty tissue in her lap.

Keep it together.

O'Connor stood and walked behind his desk with the ease of someone who belonged in rooms like this. He opened a drawer and pulled out a slip of paper. But Dee was done with paper.

"These are our counseling services," he said, sliding the page across the shiny mahogany. "We also have a chaplain on campus. He's there now. In the chapel."

Dee glanced at the page. Heat rose from her head. She imagined herself piled under a heap of paper with hundreds of numbers to call, buried alive.

O'Connor sat behind his desk. A barrier between them. His chair squeaked as he leaned forward. Trying to bridge the divide.

"We can arrange transportation," he said. "A flight. A car. Whatever you need. We can get you back to Peoria."

Back. Home. Was.

The words snagged on her like a wool sweater on a chain-link fence. Only the sweater didn't unravel as quickly as Dee.

O'Connor's face softened. "Your family will be missed at the University of Illinois."

Dee understood.

Their wallet will be missed.

She imagined him picking up the phone as soon as she left. Imagined him telling them her name. Dionne Moreland. As if that made him close to her. She imagined staying there. Walking the campus. Sitting in classrooms. Listening to professors talk about Christian cruelty and Black resistance while the real cruelty was what that eighteen-wheeler had done to her family. She imagined someone asking her, casually, weeks from now, how she was doing. She imagined herself dying to meet her family in Heaven. How she wanted to see them there now.

O'Connor broke through her dream. "We can do whatever you need."

She almost said thank you but stopped herself. She looked up at the photographs. Barack Obama's smile. The football team. The woman in pearls. Dee let her eyes linger. Her thoughts remained on her last vision: meeting her family in Heaven.

"Dionne." Concern sharpened his voice. "You don't have to do anything tonight. You don't have to go anywhere. You can stay in your dorm and rest. We can talk again tomorrow."

She planted her Moon Boots on the carpet and stood. O'Connor stood too. Her blanket slid off her shoulders. She caught it the way she hoped someone would catch her.

"My parents are dead. My sister, Rashida," she said the name slow and matter-of-fact as if spelling it out, "is dead."

O'Connor's eyebrows leaped again. "I'm so sorry."

Dee knew she could not stay inside his office any longer without screaming. She pushed the paper with crisis numbers to call right back at him with such force it gently floated to the floor. O'Connor hurried around his desk and stopped a few feet away, keeping his distance.

"Let me have someone walk you back. Let me call a counselor. Let me call someone. You shouldn't be alone."

"I don't want people."

O'Connor lifted his hands like a Black man faced with a trigger-happy cop. His voice squeaked. "I want you to know I understand you, Dionne."

She walked toward the door. Her blanket dragged behind her like a train. Fluorescent lights of the hallway buzzed overhead. As she stepped out of his office, she turned and met O'Connor's eyes. She had never raised her voice to an authority figure before. No better time to start than now.

"My name is Dee."

7

———

The prayer room sat just off the main chapel hallway. No crucifix. No Star of David. No icons, unless you counted the prayer rugs stacked up in the corner. Everything religious had been softened into something neutral. Academic and sterile yet comforting. An elevator for one.

Three narrow wooden pews sat polished and lonely. As if built for a tragedy that only affected a small handful of people. Dee stepped inside. The hair along her arms lifted. The room was dark and cool. Colder than the hallway, but nowhere near as cold as outside. Wind, sleet, and snow kamikazed themselves into Dee's eyeballs as she hurried across the quad. She wouldn't miss Illinois, just all of its memories.

The room smelled like a vintage store. Not one of the nice ones. It was musty like a moldy basement drying out.

Old people, she thought. Her grandparents were long gone, no thanks to heart attacks and diabetes. She remembered their scent, though she was young when they all passed.

I'm still young, Dee thought, balling her hands into fists.

"Hello," she called out to stop herself from thinking.

Her voice echoed throughout the tiny space. A door she hadn't noticed opened flush from the wall. The tall chaplain stepped out. Gray pants. A black short-sleeve, button-down shirt. A white priest collar. His pants fit tightly over strong, defined legs. His face was soft and smooth in a way that made Dee lower her head. She knew she looked a mess.

"Hi," he said. "I'm Gary. You must be Dee." She noticed he called her by her nickname.

Good ol' O'Connor.

Snow and slush had soaked the cuffs of her jeans on the walk over. Melted ice clung to her boots, leaving gray streaks of wet, dirty marks all over the floor. She still carried her no-longer-electric blanket around her shoulders, the fabric heavy and damp. The used tissue stayed clenched in her hand. It was as wet, gray, and dirty as what she dragged in.

"Please, sit," he said, gesturing to the pews.

She sat on the very end of the first bench. The wood was bitingly cold through her blanket since she wore no coat. The room was even darker from her seated point of view. There was no focal point to stare at other than a podium meant for preaching. It reminded her of a magician's act she once saw. The room was just as dark, though red lights were strategically placed in the corners to give off an eerie ambiance. This prayer room was eerie enough as it was. Dee's belly tugged with the possibility of magic, the same as it did watching the sleight-of-hand tricks. She hoped something impossible might happen in this room too.

The chaplain sat next to her. Three invisible bodies away.

And then there was one.

"I'm very sorry about your loss."

Dee stared ahead at the podium. She waited for him to say something more. Something meaningful. Something that might split the ceiling open with a *hallelujah.* Though she'd much prefer an *abracadabra* and a *voila!*

When the silence stretched too long, Dee said, "My parents were believers."

Gary leaned forward, pointy elbows resting on his muscular

knees. His face held sympathy. His eyes were kind, but his mouth stayed thin like a tightly pulled pink stitch.

"They were good people. Why did this happen to them?"

Gary said nothing. Now it was his time to look around at everything and nothing. Dee wanted resurrection. She wanted a Lazarus miracle. She wanted a magic that worked backward instead of up close. She imagined her mother's presence suddenly filling the room. Her father's strong hands rolling back the door like it was a heavy stone. It was too hard to imagine Rashida. That's when everything became impossibly real.

"I don't understand why I wasn't killed too."

Gary inhaled. He turned his ski slope of a nose toward the ceiling.

"Because you weren't in the car with them, Dee."

Words told to the sky came crashing down on top of her. She blinked. Waited for the rest of his sentence. Waited for a soothing psalm about the steps of a man. Our purpose in life. Walking through a dark valley. Redemption. Something. Anything. But scripture never came.

"But why'd He—"

Gary cut her off quickly. "We'll never understand God's reasons."

A creeping sense pricked at her. Like someone else was there in the room. Watching. Waiting. She didn't turn around. She studied her feet. She scuffed her boots against the floor, driving the meat of her dirty soles into the carpet, hoping to irreparably stain it so the University of Illinois would be forced to replace it.

Too bad O'Connor no longer has two generous donors to pick up the tab.

"Can I be alone now," Dee said, more as a statement than a question.

The chaplain smiled and moved toward her like he was about to pat her shoulder, then thought again.

"I'm here if you need me." He walked to his broom closet, or whatever it was, then turned back around. "We all are."

The door closed with a faint click and Dee was on her feet. The blanket dropped from her shoulders and pooled onto the pew. She stomped toward the exit, determined to burn down the school and further ruin her life.

"Achoo!"

In the far corner, balled up like a pile of dirty laundry, a shape lifted slowly. Indistinct in the low light, the figure rose from its shadow. A new sound came. The unmistakable tinkle of weeping. Dee's emotions shuffled. She landed on curiosity and squinted to see who was eavesdropping, then stopped herself.

Who cares?

She stepped in the hallway and pulled the prayer-room door shut, leaving the nosy, grieving person all to Gary. The sound of their unabashed weeping bristled her as much as being with strangers did. She wanted silence and space. Now she had no one to tell her what to do next. At least, no one she believed in.

8

———————

Before marriage, Dee thrived in solitude. But she knew up in Heaven, the Morelands worried about their baby. They'd want her to have a companion. The Bible would too. The pluck of scripture reminded her *it is not good that man be alone.*

That verse from Genesis carried her parents' voices. They'd want her to find a godly man. But Dee resisted. She wanted to stay independent. But Genesis kept rattling its chains and keeping her up at night. Even in death, Dee obeyed Morris and Mavis as she had in childhood. Reluctantly, she joined HerTrue, a Christian dating site, to find the man of her parents' dreams.

"I hope he's not *that* godly," she muttered while filling out her profile.

After a few hours on the app, Dee realized every man between thirty-three and forty-three was either married or someone she already knew. Greenup offered slim pickings. She widened her age range to thirty through forty-five. She extended her distance to include West Virginia, Louisville, even Cincinnati. Messages poured in from Jesus-loving men eager to make the drive.

Daryll was an engineer from Atlanta. He moved to Louisville to work at a tech firm with more Xs in its name than Dee thought necessary. He was tall, dark, and handsome, but asked too many questions. Some women preferred a curious conversationalist. Dee did not. Dee flipped Daryll's questions back at him, never revealing more than a few clichés.

I'm good. Life is great. Work is fun. Weather is nice. What do you think of fill-in-the-blank-to-avoid-going-any-deeper-into-my-life?

As far as Daryll knew, Dee's family was still healthy and alive. Despite a barrage of calls and texts, after their first date, Dee never spoke to him again.

Jackson wanted a big family, just like the one his mama raised. Five boys and three girls. He made that known right away. Well, right away in person. While they texted, planning his visit from Charleston, he never mentioned it once. He could have saved himself gas and bad cologne had he brought it up sooner. Dee was thirty-six and neck deep in perimenopause. Children were no longer in her future. Not that they were before. Dee didn't think herself the mothering type.

At first, she didn't hear The Change knocking on her doorstep. After her family died, her period did more than misfire. It stopped for nearly eight months. She sprained her ankle, which sidelined her runs. Weeks into recovery, her period came flooding back like the Red Sea.

While she rehabbed her body, Dee poured mental energy into her Run Café. From a pair of crutches, she built a loyal customer base. She hosted as many 5Ks and run clubs as a town of fifteen hundred couch potatoes would tolerate. She distracted herself as much as she could.

At night, after closing hours, depression engulfed her. Insomnia kept her staring at the ceiling. She clung to the promise of Psalm 30:5 — that joy would come in the morning. But each dawn broke with nothing new.

One day, after a trip to Target, Dee returned to her car and found a postcard advertising trauma therapy with Dr. Diane Heston. She pocketed it quick.

"Sometimes God tells you to see a doctor," Dr. Diane said on the phone. Dee rolled her eyes so hard she could see the wall behind her.

She tossed the flyer in the trash, laced up her trainers, and ran sixteen miles. Ankle, Dr. Diane, and the Almighty Himself could stuff it. After she'd returned to running as her sole form of therapy, her monthly bleeding faded back to spotting. Trips to the pharmacy for sanitary pads were yearly, if that.

When her periods grew even more erratic in her mid-thirties, Dee thought little of it. She only trained harder. Her first ultramarathon was a brutal fifty-miler through the Smoky Mountains. High peaks and low valleys demanded strict runner focus, but her mind wandered elsewhere and she injured herself during the race. After she earned a DNF — a runner's worst nightmare — the sloppy "did not finish" injury sent her back to PT. This time, months of rest and rehab did not reset her womanly cycle. Dee knew something was wrong.

She visited a gynecologist for the first time ever. Dr. Bruder ordered an ultrasound, found no viable eggs, and sent Dee officially from peri to pause. Motherhood vanished. Run Café became Dee's only child. All which suited Dee fine. Pregnancy required sex. At thirty-eight, Dee was still a virgin. She saved herself for marriage, as she'd been instructed. Plus, she had no desire for intimacy, biblical mandate or not. Somewhere along the way, her desire for a boyfriend died alongside her libido. She barely noticed. She finished caring about men long ago.

Of course, Dee never shared any of this with Jackson, who dreamed of starting his own Jackson 5. She handled him the same way she handled tech-bro Daryll. Eventually, he got the hint and stopped texting her too.

She refused to hand herself over to just anyone. She needed attraction and interest. She was still a queenly daughter and acted as such, even as an orphan. Dee believed loneliness was all just a part of the ride.

Until Jonas.

9

Jonas was a Kentucky boy with Kentucky swagger. He chewed toothpicks, smelled like earth, looked like charcoal, and spoke softly, like a fireman rescuing a kitten from a tree. He was gentle and humble. He reminded Dee of her father. She fell for him the instant they met.

Jonas opened doors, stood when she returned from the restroom, paid the check, and called — not texted — to confirm their date, twice. Her attraction surged but her spirit said different.

He's not the one.

She ignored the thought.

"My cousin was murdered," he said in his car.

Dee's voice cracked open. For the first time since 1999, she was ready to share.

"My parents and sister were killed by an eighteen-wheel truck."

Jonas turned to her without pity. Their eyes met, heavy with memory. Something sealed between them. Recognition. Similarity. Pain.

They barely made it through Dee's front door with all their clothes still on. Their lips crashed together. Dee yanked Jonas's shirt over his head. He unzipped her dress down to her ruby-colored panties. His calloused hands kneaded her back. Her Garmin alarm shrieked as her heart rate spiked. Dee ripped the watch off and tossed it onto the bed. His gaze stayed locked on her, hungry. But she'd never gone this far.

What do I do?

He lifted her. Pressed against her. Her body burned. Her mind raced. Her dress hung at her feet. He stepped back, sopped her in. Lust gleamed in his eyes.

Maybe we'll get married, Dee thought. *Then this won't count.*

Religious guilt barged in, late and loud.

The marital bed should be kept pure!

Her body didn't care. But Dee sure did.

"Wait." She stepped back. "I'm a virgin."

The moment shattered like a dropped dish. Jonas pulled up his pants, put on his shirt, kissed her forehead, and suggested they slow things down. Way down. He left so quick she was still standing almost all the way naked.

Humiliated and furious at herself, Dee curled under a throw blanket with a bottle of wine. She cried until sleep claimed her. Over the next few weeks, Jonas rescheduled every attempt she made at a second date. Dee filled the longing gaps with sexual fantasies and wedding daydreams.

Will it hurt? Will I orgasm? Will we get engaged the same night?

She scoured the internet, devouring stories from teenage first-timers. Blood. Pain. Babies. Dee wondered if menopause stopped hymens from bleeding, but no testimonies were there.

Weeks stretched into months. His replies shrank to one word: *sorry.* Then nothing. After nine weeks, Jonas vanished. Dee disabled the HerTrue app, letting cobwebs settle over her love life as well as the pristine vaginal membrane she'd keep forever, mad at herself for ever trying.

About a year later, on her way to the Barcelona Marathon, Dee watched well-dressed Spanish men board her plane. Desire rose again within her, familiar, now welcome. As a dashing caramel-colored man took his seat next to her, suddenly, her ego miraculously healed.

An hour into the flight, her seatmate dozed off. She logged onto the Wi-Fi and reactivated HerTrue, hoping to meet men like the one next to her. She changed her profile status from *devout* to *somewhat religious*. She didn't want the next guy thinking she was some prude. She'd leave with no aftermath. No courtesy call. Ghosting before there was a name for it.

This way I can't get attached.

In Spain, she toured Gaudí with an Antonio Banderas looka-like. In Montana, she drank moonshine with a cattle rancher. In London, she strolled Hyde Park with a West End actor. She flirted expertly, remained mysterious and low maintenance. She didn't want anything more than a good, wholesome time.

She shunned anyone who tried to get close. "I'm leaving tomorrow" became her favorite truth. With no strings attached, Dee dated like a divorced middle-aged man in a midlife crisis — minus the sports car and sex.

Dee used the app to her advantage. She perfected the art of leaving first. The tactic long suited her. Until one trip to Canada when it completely failed.

10

———

Dee flew north for the International Marathon that spanned from Michigan to Ontario. For the first time ever, she didn't study the course map. Her mind was focused on other things. Other *men*. Rejection was something that no longer stung.

Plenty of Canadian men swiped right on her profile. She saw okay matches in Windsor, but it wasn't until Toronto that she found a more promising variety of men to try.

Dee settled into her hotel room, eager for a hot bath. She ordered a room-service appetizer sampler, the same as her approach to dating. She swiped right on a lumberjack. A Mountie. An NHL goalie. She wanted to fill her calendar before she filled the bathtub. Two a day would produce ten dates during her visit. She hoped a few would offer insider city tours. Perhaps others would elicit flirtatious attractions, no matter how fleeting they may be.

As she finally closed out of the app, something inside her said, *just one more.*

Dee opened HerTrue to find a White man holding a chubby pug on his lap.

I'll never pick up poop.

Then she read the caption. The dog belonged to a friend.

Curiosity nudged her even further. She explored the profile. Camping. Guitars. Hockey. Swiping left was probably best. But Dee paused at the final photo. Her finger hovered above the man, his arm around what appeared to be his mother, not an older ex. An assumption that was confirmed with his profile prompt:

Which deceased person would you want to have dinner with?

His answer: *My mom.*

Dee's finger swiped right. Eric Taylor matched with her almost instantly. Back home, she would have blown off his eagerness. Here, she was thankful. She didn't have time to waste.

She made no effort to hide her temporary presence. Anyone who read her profile could learn the hard facts:

I live full-time in Kentucky and am here on a short vacation.

But most men didn't read her profile. They discovered her through conversation only. Eric, however, studied up. He asked thoughtful questions: *Where are your favorite races? Is the grass really blue in Kentucky?* He even recognized a yellow poplar in one of her photos. In Canada, the tree was highly valued for everything from cabins to construction. Eric's work mirrored Dee's father. Like Morris, he was a builder himself.

They met at the Reservoir Lounge at seven. Night slid into morning without either noticing. They planned to see each other the next (same) day at the famous jazz club, the Rex Hotel. Dee rarely, if ever, saw her travel dates twice. But Eric proved fascinating, attentive, and kind. Plus, he liked jazz. Just like her dad. She agreed to see Eric again.

Date two was spent table dancing to a live trio. Afterward, Eric walked Dee to her hotel. He pointed at the almost-full moon.

"Would you like to watch the Hunter Moon rise tomorrow night with a Canadian?"

She only understood half of what he was talking about but said yes anyway. Even standing next to him, she couldn't wait for date three.

The restaurant atop the CN Tower had a spectacular view of the full Hunter Moon. They ended the night with a walk along the Toronto harborfront. Eric balanced talking and listening. He respected her boundaries. He didn't ask too many personal questions. Dee was prepared to barricade herself against private feelings or past wounds. Shunning her own personal space, she asked about Eric's deceased mother instead.

He hesitated, then pulled out his phone. "That's her in my profile," he said, scrolling to the photo. She had kind eyes. Wind-tossed hair. Her arm was slung around him. Both of them squinted into the sun.

"She used to come to all my hockey games," he said, smiling. "She'd yell at the ref by calling him 'stripes.'"

Dee waited for tears and hoped hers wouldn't follow.

"I really miss her," he added, then put his phone away. Dee was surprised he didn't cry when talking about his mom in the past tense.

I wonder if I'll ever get there, she thought.

Eric changed the subject and asked Dee what she looked for in a partner. She laughed, shrugged, and said, "I travel too much for commitment."

His body betrayed his disappointment. She asked him the same question to be polite.

"I want someone who makes me think. I like to be challenged. Well, sort of." He laughed. "Losing my mom was challenging enough." Dee understood. "It sounds crazy, but I guess since we met on a Christian app, I can say it: It's important my wife believes in God. Or the universe. Or whatever. That really helped me after... you know. My mom."

Dee bit her lip. She never considered marriage, really. But for the first time since she'd joined HerTrue, Dee wondered if the man she was with could be something more than just a travel date, because Eric felt safe.

"Can I kiss you?" Dee asked, her ears burning at her own question.

Eric was just as shocked as she was. "Yes. Please."

The kiss proved sweet and tender. Enough to keep Dee

thinking about it. Later, in her hotel room, Dee found herself missing someone she barely knew.

Date four brought them to Halton, outside Toronto, hiking to Rattlesnake Point. Eric packed a picnic: macaroni salad with homemade carrot cake, one of Dee's favorites. They kept conversation light, savoring the previous night's kiss and avoiding vulnerability. They both knew time was running out.

Say something, they silently urged each other.

Outside Dee's hotel, sadness creased at the corner of two sets of eyes as they planned their final evening together.

What are we doing? they wondered.

As Dee rode the seven lonely flights up to her room, her phone pinged. She'd turned off HerTrue notifications long ago, so that wasn't it. This was a text from someone she'd already been conversing with.

"Can you come back down a sec?" it read.

Dee pressed the elevator button so hard she broke her nail. Eric waited in the lobby, barely containing himself. Before she could speak, he spilled his soul all over the Royal York's yellow poplar floor.

"I don't want tonight to be the last time we see each other. I really like you."

Dee's eyes sparkled. "I really like you too."

It surprised her that she actually meant it.

11

———

Eric noticed it immediately: the way Dee broke eye contact before she decided whether to be vulnerable. It wasn't flirtation, exactly. It was more like stepping into a sudden protective shield.

She laughed easily, asked good questions, thanked him for small things like holding a door, choosing a place, or picking up the check. She leaned forward when she spoke. Then leaned back again when she listened. The space between them was fluid and evolving.

At first, Eric took her to places where the atmosphere would do the talking. A bustling lounge. A jazz trio. Locations soft enough to converse, but loud enough for silence.

On their first date, Dee wore a dress that fit her personality. An angled, tight thing that didn't reveal too much. She smelled clean, like soap and citrus. She sat across from him with her hands folded around her drink, which she sipped slow.

"So," she said, putting down her cocktail. "Tell me what I should know about Toronto."

Eric laughed. "That depends. How much time do you have here?"

Her eyes flicked away, then she smiled. "I leave pretty soon."

He told her about neighborhoods he liked, restaurants he

frequented, music he listened to. She asked follow-ups. She was attentive and disarming. Most people waited their turn to speak. Dee collected details like a detective hunting down clues.

She talked about running. About travel. About Kentucky, briefly. Eric clocked what she left out as much as what she shared. She spoke in finished sentences and rarely circled back. No loose ends. No fishing. No vulnerable cracks.

They shut down the Reservoir Lounge, the last to leave. Later, walking her back to the hotel, Eric pointed out the moon high over the buildings, nearly full.

"Would you like to watch the Hunter Moon rise tomorrow with a Canadian?"

She looked up, squinting. "The what moon go where with who?" The two laughed. She didn't need an explanation. She simply said, "Yes. I like how you talk."

He opened at that. It was a compliment like his mom would've given.

Use your words, she'd tell him. *You're good with words.*

Outside Dee's hotel, they stretched out their time. Dee shifted her weight from one foot to the other, key already in hand. But she didn't leave.

Their next night together, Eric noticed the pulsation of risk behind his ribs. Not so much danger as a pang of possibility. The wisp of a relationship despite logistics and truth.

He noticed how often she glanced at her watch. How she framed stories around departures, flights, checkouts, and finish lines. He didn't mistake it for disinterest. He recognized that too.

Walking along the harbor, they kept things light. Both of them knew an ending was imminent. They didn't want to bruise it by naming it. There was seriousness under the ease.

"Can I kiss you?" she asked, throwing him for a loop. As much as he wanted her, he didn't know until that moment that she felt the same way.

Their kiss was gentle and generous. Neither lingering nor rushed. The familiar poke of his past rose up between his legs.

I will not mess this up by going too fast.

The next date, a hike and a lunch he prepared. Their conversation light, yet heavy. She was leaving tomorrow and there still was so much to explore.

After dropping her at her hotel to get ready for their last dinner together, Eric defaulted to urgency. He had to say something. Yes, they were different, but perhaps she'd see past it.

"I don't want tomorrow to be the last time we see each other." His eagerness was out in the open. "I really like you."

Dee's eyebrows smoothed out from a confused V to a soft line.

"I really like you too," she said.

Eric believed her. He also believed she might ghost him. Distance, risk, his past. He didn't ignore the calculations. He didn't let them decide the outcome either. Dee was worth taking a chance.

After their second kiss, he stepped from the lobby into the night air on wobbly knees. The moon shone down on him, bright and unashamed of its gravitational pull.

12

After her shower and time spent dabbing alcohol on her wounds, Dee drove to Run Café, unlocked the door, and flipped the CLOSED sign to OPEN. She operated from 8 until 5. Sometimes earlier or later depending on how she felt. Today, she felt awful and considered not coming in. She was surprised the door was still locked when she got there. She figured Madison had already opened for the day but she was nowhere in sight.

The bell above the door tinkled. A couple in red-and-black flannels stepped in, a baby strapped to the woman's chest, the man glued to his phone.

"Are you open?"

Dee's eyes flicked to the sign. "Yes."

"What's your Wi-Fi?"

"No Wi-Fi. We're not that kind of store."

The man lifted his head to take in the empty café. "What kind of store are you?"

"For runners."

"Never mind."

They walked out as quick as they'd come. The bell signaled their departure.

Red-and-black flannel. Amanda. That day.

Dee sighed as she watched them walk next door.

Run Café sat at the end of the strip mall Eric called the Mini Mall Marketplace. A three-unit structure wedged between Dollar General and Barney's Pharmacy. Dee employed one person, Madison Wheelock, who wore such a tight bun it made her look stern. And stern she was. Madison had handled the books ever since the café opened. She didn't believe in its success.

"It's not a sustainable model," Madison would often tell Dee. "You're losing more money than you're bringing in. I don't even know how you can afford to pay me."

Dee would only roll her eyes and ignore Madison's review.

Once Eric received his EAD card allowing him to legally work in the States, Greenup High hired him as its hockey coach. He loved the sport so much he not only coached it, but also played with an old-timers' club. Dee was happy he made friends. He had way more than she did. Because Greenuppers had plumbing to fix, leaves to rake, gutters to clean, Dee was also grateful for the random handyman jobs Eric took on here and there. Anything to keep him out of the house.

A heap of mail sat on the counter. Dee ignored the grocery circulars and generic envelopes addressed to "resident." Glossy mailers announced upcoming marathons, 5Ks, and Tough Mudder obstacle courses. One flyer caught her eye: an elite 100K ultramarathon in the Blue Ridge Mountains near Roanoke, Virginia. Dee once ran the grueling Blue Ridge Marathon. The two-mile uphill climb alone surpassed anything she ever trained for. She couldn't imagine tackling 100K over those same hills. Runners would face an elevation change of over 7,000 feet.

Dee noted the date of the race and scoffed.

Never. At least not trained for those hills in less than a year.

Her eyes landed on the $20,000 cash prize for the men's winner and $15,000 for the women. She tossed the flyer in with the rest of the trash, announcing one word:

"Misogyny."

She unlocked the café's safe using the combination 05-21-19, an abbreviated version of Rashida's birthday, who would've turned forty in a month. For Rashida's thirtieth, Dee had written an anonymous check to Peoria High. It was big enough to make the principal cry. She saw pictures in the paper for proof. This year, her checkbook would have to stay closed.

Dee grabbed the money pouch holding $200 in small bills for the register. Just in case someone used cash.

Just in case someone came in.

The bag was light. She unzipped it. But there were no cash and no receipts. It was empty.

"What in the...?"

Dee pulled out her phone and called Madison. The phone rang until a robot asked her to leave a message. Madison's own voice was her usual outgoing prompt. Dee couldn't remember a time when Madison ever used a generic message.

"Mad, there's no money in the money pouch. Call me back."

She ended the call. *Madison stole it.* She shook her head clear. *Madison never took money without telling me.*

Dee wavered between judgment and grace. Her default system kicked in. *Forgive us our trespasses as we forgive those who trespass against us.* But biblical verses about forgiveness failed to cool Dee's rising temper. Her thumbs moved instead.

"Did you take my money from my cash drawer?"

She hit send on the text and waited for bubbles, but none came. After minutes spent staring and waiting, she left the empty sack on the counter and flipped the light switch. No lights came on. She toggled the switch on and off. It was the same result as the sack: nothing.

"What now?"

On the counter, a vintage cash register sat under a dust cloth. Next to it, a card reader, though Dee always pushed cash.

"But no one uses cash anymore," Dee said aloud, mocking a former customer's comment.

With the lights, the device, and her thoughts going dark, Dee concluded the electricity was officially out. She opened the café door, ringing the bell overhead, and hurried next door to Collar's Greens — an eco-friendly pet store she never patronized since she owned no pets. Through the bay window, Dee saw Larry, the owner, restocking shelves beneath bright ceiling lights reflecting off his shiny bald head. Techno music thumped from speakers. Dee pushed open the door.

"Did your electricity go out?"

Larry clutched a Kong toy with a gasp. "What? No. Why?"

Dee neither answered nor wanted to. Larry loved gossip. She left Collar's without a word and rushed back to her café. The bell announced her return as she stormed into the back room, straight to the electrical box. She opened the metal panel and flipped a breaker. Still nothing. She pulled out her phone and tapped Eric's contact.

"Hey, sweet -- I -- about -- you," Eric's warm voice crackled through the spotty reception that irritated customers and Madison alike.

"My power's out." Dee noticed she skipped a greeting. "Hi," she croaked, hoping that would suffice.

"Did -- check -- eakers?"

"Yes! I tried the breakers. Larry's power's on and mine's not," she whined.

"I don't know what else to do," Eric said. "It -- come back --"

Dee's eyes narrowed. *Why'd I call him?*

Her Garmin blared, assuming she was overexerting herself on a run.

"Sounds like -- rate up. You -- ay?"

"No, I'm not okay. I don't know what's going on with my power!" Dee wedged her phone between shoulder and ear to silence the alarm.

"You call -- ower company?"

"Oh, duh. No. I'll call you back," Dee said.

"Wait! I want -- you -- something."

Eric always stretched conversations when she wanted to end them.

"I can't talk right now. I got a lot going on."

This time, Eric came through clearly. "Ooh, customers?"

"I think Madison stole from me, okay?!"

"WHAT? When? Are -- sure?"

"Tell you later. Bye." She pressed the red end-call button and hung up.

It was mean, but once everything's fixed, I'll apologize. Maybe we can have make up—

Dee banished the rest of her thought. She stuck out her tongue, disgusted. She wanted to love sex, and assumed Eric did too. But by the time they married, her libido had disappeared and the thought of the act made her gag.

She pushed her mind free and googled the electric company's number on her phone's sluggish internet. When Kentucky Power's contact page finally loaded, Dee pressed call and paced the café, hunting for a signal. Finally, she found a spot facing a wall with three bars instead of one.

A long, recorded message about tornadoes greeted her. Sunshine streamed outside. Weather wasn't responsible for this outage. Eventually, the robotic menu began.

"Press 1 for billing, press 2 for new clients, press 3 for existing clients, press 4 for—"Dee pressed 3. Hillbilly muzak filled the line. Banjos and fiddles played an instrumental version of "My Sharona" by The Knack. After two rounds of the chorus, a customer service agent answered.

"This is Angela. How can I help you today?"

Dee wanted to yell but restrained herself.

"Dionne Moreland Taylor. 1523 Thoroughbred Lane, number 101. Zip 41444. I don't know the account number," she said.

"Let me pull your information up." Angela's calm, patient tone soothed Dee's spiraling. Dee closed her eyes, coming closer to prayer than she'd managed in a long time.

Angela gasped.

"What's wrong?"

"Your payment's overdue."

"When was it due?" Dee never had an overdue account before.

"The twenty-second of every month," Angela said. Dee checked her phone. It wasn't even the 15th. Before Dee could say as such, Angela's voice hardened. "Your power was shut off because you haven't paid your bill in six months."

"WHAT?! That's impossible!"

The bell over the door jingled. Dee turned and saw Martin. Her landlord hadn't stopped by in years. She studied him. Stress or alcoholism showed in his bloodshot eyes and deep bags.

Maybe he's here to tell me he's dying.

As Dee stepped toward him, her phone lost connection.

"Power -- due balance," Angela's voice crackled.

Dee waved Martin to wait and moved back to the wall for a signal. "How much?"

"-- hous -- ollars."

Did she say thousand?

"What'd you say? You broke up."

"Four thousand dollars. Make that payment in full, and your power will be restored."

Dee dropped the phone.

Four thousand dollars?!

Martin picked up Dee's phone and handed it to her. "I wish you would've told me you were having a problem sooner."

At the word *problem*, Dee's mind went everywhere except money.

"Maybe we could've worked something out. But I could've come by earlier myself. It's just as much my fault, I guess."

Dee frowned.

"What happened to your eye?" he asked.

Dee touched the bruise. "I tripped." She kept her voice calm. "What problem of mine are you referring to?"

"Your rent, Dee. You haven't paid me in six months."

13

———

Dee floored the gas pedal of her hybrid Hyundai toward home. On the Bluetooth speaker, another call to Madison rang and rang. Madison's bland "please leave a message" came over the car's speaker.

"Call me back already! Is this your fault?!" Dee hung up and immediately called again.

How could she steal from me? Right under my nose!

Dee pulled onto the long, gravelly turnoff to her home. Instead of feeling the welcoming hug her property usually gave her, a lingering sense of dread settled in.

What else did she take?

Dee bolted from her Hyundai so fast she left the driver's door open. Thankfully, Eric was at work. She didn't have the where-withal to explain what was happening.

Though it would be nice to have someone calm me down.

Her mind raced. Her heart pounded. She ripped off her watch so it wouldn't sound the alarm every five seconds. Once inside, she grabbed her laptop and opened it, relieved when the Wi-Fi signal appeared in the corner.

All's good here. So far...

Dee logged into her bank accounts. She had three — Run

Café, her personal checking and savings that held her inheritance, and a newer joint account with Eric. The combined total was just above $220,000.

Eric still kept his Canadian account with his own dwindling inheritance. Dee never thought about his money. Now she desperately needed it. Instead of a six-figure balance in her accounts, she stared at a number with only three.

"TWO HUNDRED DOLLARS?!"

Dee's fingers flew across the keyboard. She scanned withdrawals. Zelle transfers. Payments. All sent to Madison Cotto.

I thought her last name was Wheelock?

The dates stretched way back. Small amounts. Big ones. Then huge. Madison paid herself through Dee's accounts. She filed Dee's taxes. She knew Dee's social security number. She checked her mail. She fielded calls. She got the bills. Dee gave Madison access to everything. Dee was the one who handed over full control of her finances.

Now all of it's gone!

And so was Madison.

14

———

The police station was small and cramped. Molded plastic chairs were bolted to the floor. A bulletin board hung with flyers about lost dogs. A young cadet sat behind the counter, flipping through a stack of forms. His uniform looked stiff, like it hadn't been broken in yet.

"I need to file a report," Dee said.

The cadet blinked. "What kind of report?"

"Theft. Fraud." She hesitated, then added, "I was robbed."

"Oh." He sat up straighter. "Okay." He reached under the counter and pulled out a clipboard. "Have a seat."

She didn't. She watched his pen scratch, his letters slow and careful.

"Your name?"

"Dionne Moreland Taylor."

"And who was stolen from?"

"Me."

He nodded, then frowned at the next line. "Do you know the person who robbed you?"

"Madison Wheelock."

"Relationship?"

"My bookkeeper."

He glanced up. "How long has she been working for you?"

The question landed hard. The answer was harder.

"Twenty-two years." Dee balled her fists. "Since I moved here, basically."

The cadet's eyebrows lifted as he wrote slow. "Twenty-two years." He slid the clipboard toward her. "I'll need you to fill the rest of this out."

The pen was cheap plastic. The paper smelled like bleach. On the clipboard, a million little empty boxes lay beneath her name and Madison's.

DATE OF INCIDENT

Dee stared at the line. "It wasn't one day," she said. "She'd been stealing." The cadet looked at her blankly. "Over years. Little amounts over time."

"Okay. How much are we talking?"

"Two hundred and twenty thousand dollars. Maybe more."

"That's... wow. Sorry." Perspiration dabbed at the sparse mustache above his lip.

Dee's eyes narrowed. She opened her folder and slid bank statements across the counter. He flipped through them, lips moving silently. Numbers, dates, transfers.

"All to the same name," he said.

"Yes."

He frowned. "I thought you said Wheelock."

Dee's stomach dropped. "I did."

He turned the page over. "This says Cotto."

"That's not her name."

He typed something into his ancient computer with his lone pointer finger. The screen reflected in his eyes. "It could be her married name."

"She wasn't married."

The cadet cleared his throat. "Maybe you didn't know. It sounds like—" He stopped himself. Dee went stiff and embarrassed all at once.

Chapter 14

Twenty-two years and I didn't know the name attached to my money.

"I need to tell you upfront, cases like this are hard to prosecute."

"Why?"

"Because these are all authorized transfers from you through your account."

"No, I—"

"Even if you didn't mean to authorize them, they look legit. We'll file the report. But the bank handles recovery."

"But my money's all gone," Dee said slowly.

"Yes, ma'am."

"And she's gone."

"If she's left the state, that complicates matters."

"So, nothing happens?"

"Not nothing," he said, tapping the clipboard. "It's documented." He reached into a drawer and pulled out a card. "If you hear from her, or if anything else changes, call us."

She took the card. It weighed less than a one-dollar bill.

"That's it?" She blinked.

"For now."

She walked out, refusing to cry in the station. In the parking lot, however, Dee sat in her car and let the tears fall.

15

———

Eric gripped the steering wheel and stared at the bank's text on his phone. He'd tried to talk to Dee about it earlier, but she'd cut him off again. The same way she did whenever she needed him, then didn't. He didn't want to worry her further while she dealt with the power outage. But he had no idea how to make her listen.

Dee does whatever she wants, regardless of what I need.

She never called him back about the electricity. She never called him with problems. Dee never rested. She was on the go constantly. Even when he got her alone, she kept moving.

Eric's phone buzzed again. Another low-balance alert from their new American bank. Low-balance alerts only triggered when the account dipped below five figures. He could've checked the account from his phone, but Dee didn't like mobile banking. She called it dangerous. He never had a problem in Canada, but here he always did whatever she wanted.

The alert wasn't true. It couldn't be. In the past month, he'd taken $200,000 CAD, the rest of his inheritance, and transferred it into their joint account. He saw how much she was spending on who knows what. He figured she — and their account — could use a boost.

He turned onto Dee's driveway. The house didn't quite feel

like his home yet. Sometimes Dee still called it hers. Either way, he was a visitor. Their home was not "theirs."

A police cruiser sat behind Dee's car. Eric's stomach tightened. He parked, shoved the van door open, and sprinted toward her house.

"DEE?!" he yelled as he entered.

He barreled into the living room. Two cops stood on either side of the room. Dee slumped on the sofa, wiping away tears.

Eric exhaled. *She's here, safe.*

"Who's that?" one policeman asked.

"My husband." Dee blew her nose with a honk.

Eric focused on her face. "What happened to your eye?"

"She fell," the other officer grunted.

"Are you okay?" Eric sat next to Dee and wrapped an arm around her.

"That's not why they're here." She shrugged him off. "Madison drained our bank accounts."

Eric processed quickly. "We'll be okay if that's true."

Dee swung from despair to fury in an instant. She kicked the tissue box across the floor. The two cops quickly exited the room.

"It is true! That's why the power was off! She hasn't paid Martin my rent in six months!"

"Six months? Gosh, that's... that's how long we've been married."

Dee's eyes widened. Clarity crossed her face. "She knew I never paid any attention to the bank. Maybe she assumed my new husband would watch more closely. She had to move fast and drain the accounts before *you noticed*!" She jabbed a finger at Eric. "This is because of you!"

Eric flinched. *She needs someone to blame and I'm the only one here.*

She opened her laptop. "Transfer me twenty thousand dollars."

He gulped. "I don't have twenty thousand to transfer. If Madison took that money, she took my inheritance too."

16

———————

Eric lay on the bed with his eyes closed, his hands clasped over his stomach. The pressure on his belly calmed him. He was on his side of the mattress. Dee wasn't on hers.

Who knows when she will be again.

Her heavy footsteps moved through the house. In the kitchen, down the hall, back again. A drawer slammed. The front door opened. Each movement erratic and jarring. Eric inhaled through his nose. Counted. Held. Released. Box breathing for when things got too big. Same with prayer.

Help her. Help us. Help me know what to say.

He opened his eyes as Dee passed the bedroom doorway without looking in, her body language just as tight as hours prior. He almost called out to her but decided against it. He closed his eyes again and imagined pulling his wife close and telling her everything would be okay. That he had this. That they could handle it. That she wasn't alone. He imagined she believed him. A silvery peace flanked by forgiveness. Then her loud footsteps woke his daydream. She entered the bedroom. The floorboards creaked. Eric stayed still and triggered. He was afraid if he moved, she'd yell at him again. Or worse.

Chapter 16

Tell me what to do, he prayed.

Nothing happened. Dee kept moving. The nightstand. The closet. The bathroom. Gone.

Eric tightened his hands over his belly, resisting the urge to get up and urinate like before.

17

Eric lay in bed in cowboy pajamas. His blanket with rocket ships and bright planets was tucked high and tight underneath his chin. His little hands rested on his tummy as he held himself close.

The house clicked from a wood furnace. Pipes knocked behind walls. His dark room held the faint sweetness of his mom's perfume. A scent left over from a bedtime story about a prince and princess whose love story he liked but knew was make-believe.

His ears perked up as the heavy oak door creaked open and slammed closed. Hard leather shoes scraped across hand-laid tile. His four-year-old heart fluttered. His lost butterfly escaped into his chest once again.

His father's voice slurred through the hall. "Hello? Who's awake?"

Eric slid from under the wool blanket. He padded to his bedroom door and cracked it open. His mom's perfume quickly doused by the smell of pungent spoiled apples.

Howard swayed in place in the hallway, fur coat still on. Hair mussed. Cheeks flushed. A smear of red marked the corner of his mouth. Lipstick. Not his mom's color.

A hinge squeaked. The door across the hall opened. "You're going to wake him up," Eric's mom whispered.

Chapter 17

"Nonsense. He sleeps like a rock," Howard slurred, then raised his voice. "Ain't that right, kiddo?"

Eric's stomach dropped. He pulled his door closed, no longer able to see.

He's going to come in here.

Eric hurried to his bed, almost losing his balance. He threw back his covers and shoved himself inside. He tried to remember what he was supposed to do when his dad came home like this. Sometimes Dad was funny. Sometimes he was loud. Sometimes he was angry. Very angry. Eric could never rely on any one thing.

He closed his eyes and counted his breathing like his mom had taught him to do whenever he got scared. He wished his dad knew how to count breaths too.

Maybe it'd help him remember to be nice.

"Let the boy sleep," Eric's mom warned.

But it was too late. Howard was already in the door.

"How you doin', son?" His sour breath filled the room. "What'd you have for supper?"

He plopped himself on the bed, making Eric's small body lift mid-air for a single instant.

I'm free.

As Eric fell back to earth, his heart kept going. Thudding as if it hadn't landed. He focused on keeping his eyelids closed. Blobs of gunk swirled and swam behind them. Howard's shadow moved closer. Eric tried to make himself disappear. But Howard's hot breath was on him. The trick never worked.

"Come on, Howie, go wash up," Mom said.

Howard pulled away from her with enough force to shake the mattress. "I'm clean, Joanne," he said. "Well, not that kind of clean."

"You have lipstick all over your face." Her voice was small. Forgotten.

Eric opened his eyes.

"There you are." Howard leaned in, his breath stinking and stinging.

"Hi Dad."

"Howard." His mom was stern now. "He doesn't need to see you like this."

"Relax. I was only out with the guys."

Eric shifted in bed. All three knew it was a lie.

"Fine. I won't do it again, okay?" He looked at Eric. "I won't drink. I won't look at other women." Howard turned to the ceiling. "I promise you, God. I'm done with all of that stuff!"

Joanne dropped her head. She'd heard it before. "Good. Now let's let our son sleep."

Eric's eyes widened, waiting for whatever it was Howard would do next. It never seemed to be the same thing twice.

"Okay." Howard yawned. "I'm beat."

His girth lifted from the mattress, rolling Eric back into place. Howard dragged himself out, shutting off the light, forgetting his wife and child were still in the room, wide awake.

The house went still again. Except for its old squeaks. Eric waited to see if his dad would come back and yell or make his mom cry again. When none of that happened, his body loosened and his underwear pooled with pee.

He knew his dad wouldn't remember what he'd said. If he did, he'd break his promises as usual. Eric wanted to help his dad get better, but he didn't know how.

"He doesn't mean it," Eric told his mom as her perfume fought the scent of urine.

"I disagree," Joanne said, lifting Eric from his wet pajamas, her hands warm and smooth. She remade his bed with sheets made up of hockey players and flying pucks. "So, we're going to let him prove it to us his own way. Okay?"

Eric wanted to argue, but he couldn't, and wouldn't, raise his voice to his mom. "Okay."

Joanne put her hands over Eric's, now under new, clean sheets. "I love you."

"I love you too."

But by the time he said it, she was already back in her room.

18

———

Eric and Joanne knew just where to step, stop for water, and rest along the Staircase to Heaven Trail. The breathtaking route cut up through swaths of yellow poplars just outside Elmira, Ontario. It placed them atop of Bruce's Peak with a view steep enough to steal your breath away.

While the rest of town bowed their heads indoors, Joanne and Eric plodded forward for their regularly scheduled Sunday excursion. Despite the decade and a half since they started hiking this path, Joanne's pace never slowed. Eric's hockey-toned body adjusted its stride to match hers, though his knees and ankles told him to slow down.

Joanne wore a long skirt to hide her swollen calves. Her sensible shoes wore smooth at the heel. It was beyond time for new ones, though she didn't agree. Nor would she let Eric spend his money. She'd rather he put it toward college. A conversation that was forever on hold.

Eric watched his mom dab sweat from her brow. Part hot flash, part altitude change. Joanne never complained. She walked determined, her steps deliberate and careful.

The two passed large families heading down their same path.

Men in pressed shirts. Women in skirts like Joanne's. Well-behaved, towheaded children holding elders' sleeves.

Joanne smiled, but the Mennonites never smiled back. The Taylor family was no longer part of their flock.

"What's this one's name again?" Joanne asked Eric. "I can never keep them straight."

"Julia." He beamed. "And she's gorgeous."

"I can tell." His mom laughed at the mischievous twinkle in her son's eye. "What do you like so much about her?"

"Uhhh." Eric stopped to think. "The fact that she wants me?"

Joanne threw her head back and cackled, not breaking her stride. "They all want you."

Eric regained his footing. "True."

"What is it *you* want?"

Instead of pausing to answer, Eric kept his mom's pace, mouth closed.

I want to be wanted.

He didn't say how desperate his wanting was. His mom wouldn't understand. She was a good listener, never interrupting, always asking questions. But sometimes he wasn't sure she heard what he said.

"Do you want to marry her?"

Now it was Eric's turn to laugh. "Heck no! I don't like her like that."

"You never do. But you will one day."

"I highly doubt it."

"I don't. You will want to marry. You'll know when you meet her."

Eric rolled his eyes.

"Just remember, marriage is ten percent love and ninety percent commitment," she said, almost casually.

"Horseradish." Eric frowned. Joanne kept moving uphill. "If love isn't there, what's the point?" He summoned confidence to continue. "Why be miserable forever?"

Chapter 18

Joanne expected this answer. "Love changes. Commitment stays."

Another Mennonite family passed without eye contact. Joanne stepped to the side to let them by. Eric did not.

"Why stay in a relationship that's not worth staying in?"

Joanne's gaze slid from the Mennonites and landed on her son. She'd been waiting for this conversation. Now it was here.

"Eric, leaving is easy. Staying is what's hard."

"That's why you stayed with Dad? Because it was hard?"

Joanne let her eyelids close, breaking eye contact. "Yes."

Eric shook his head. "That's not fair to anyone. Especially you." He passed his mom on the trail and pushed his way up the hill. Joanne tried to stay fast on his heels.

They kept climbing wordlessly. His legs hurt. He was light-headed. The butterfly was out of his ribcage, but he didn't slow.

She should've left him. Why didn't she? He was awful.

The words pressed against Eric's teeth, sharp and ready.

I hate him.

Or maybe it was *I hate what he did to us.* Or *I hate who I am because of him.* The sentence wouldn't settle. *I hate him* stuck.

Dead leaves crunched behind him. Joanne's breathing was heavier. She caught up, hand braced on her heart. She kept her eyes on the trail. On where best to fall in case she passed out.

Eric opened his mouth to tell his mom what he'd decided. "You should hate—"

Joanne captured his eye, quick and hopeful. Ready to receive whatever he offered.

"Use your words." She took a gasp of air. "You're good with your words."

But Eric held them. He saw an exhausted woman. One without complaint. If he said his emotions and feelings out loud, they wouldn't land on Howard. They would land on her.

"I don't want to be like him," he said instead.

"You can still love someone even if they hurt you."

Eric spat his words over his shoulder. "That keeps you stuck."

"Sometimes being stuck is better than being alone."

"You should've left him," he said, immediately wishing he could take his words back.

Nice job, asshole, he told himself.

"I couldn't. I was pregnant."

Eric flinched like he'd been slapped. The smell of his mom's perfume landed on him before her soft hand did. "I should have, I know. But I had to think of you."

Her hand slipped into the crook of his elbow. Shoulder to top of head, they walked arm in arm up the crest of the hill without speaking. Eric's chest felt tight, not from the climb or the butterfly or the Mennonites who shunned them, but from his mom. He wanted to fix her. To debate a past long gone. He wanted to give her a better life than the one she'd built. But she wasn't asking for answers. She only needed Eric to know why she stayed.

At the top, the trail leveled out to a flat opening where Elmira and all its heavy memories sprawled out before them. Side by side, they took in their town. The church steeples. The yellow poplars. The simple order of life. Joanne breathed it in.

"It all makes sense when you look at it from up here, eh?"

"Yeah." Eric blinked back a tear. "It does."

19

Tanya stood in the doorway of the kitchen, arms crossed, voice high and pointed. Fighting about money. Planning what happened next now that Joanne was gone.

"You can't keep pretending she's still here," Tanya yelled. "You need to think about the future. *Our* future."

Eric stared at his work boots. The heels were wearing out. He couldn't explain why, but he couldn't bring himself to buy another pair.

"I am thinking about the future," he mumbled. "It doesn't look like the one you want."

"What's that supposed to mean?"

Why am I in this? Why stay?

Tanya growled, frustrated by his attention on everything but her. "Just sell the damn house already!" She gestured vaguely, as if to say not the house they were standing in. The one Eric bought himself after getting a good job as the facilities attendant at the hockey rink that afforded him the ability to buy a home only two blocks away from his mom. "She's been gone for three months. We could use the money."

"I don't want to sell it, okay? There are too many memories there."

Tanya laughed, but it wasn't kind. "I thought you hated your childhood."

Eric winced. *You should know better than to bring that up.*

He drove without thinking, ending up two towns over at the Lumberjack, like he had a hundred times before. Here, no one asked questions about inheritances or real estate or childhood trauma. Here, everyone saw each other through the bottom of a shot glass. Blurry and fun.

He drank too fast. Let a woman press her mouth against his. Then another. And quite possibly a third. He never went home with them. Not in the past few months or so, at least. They were a distraction. A quick fix. An inherited addiction.

Instead of going home to Tanya, he drove back to the squeaky old house that told bedtime stories without ever saying a word. He kicked off his boots and swayed in the hallway, drunk and stinky. Just like his dead old dad.

Eric reached for the light switch and missed it. When the hallway finally brightened, he found his reflection in the narrow mirror by the door. He leaned closer, squinting. A faint red smudge marked the edge of his mouth. Lipstick. Not Tanya's color. He rubbed it with his thumb.

The smell hit him next. Sour beer, sweat, perfume that wasn't his girlfriend's. Apples gone bad. Eric pressed both hands to the sink and stared hard at himself. His eyes glassy. His face sunken. He looked older and acted younger. He put the night together in pieces. Barstool. Laughter. Women who felt good. The hollow ride home.

He never planned to kiss anyone. It just happened. Like the pull of gravity. Eric rubbed the color away from his face. His heart tightened. The butterfly fluttered. A memory surfaced. His father in the hallway. Fur coat still on. The vacant look in his eyes. The same careless promise waiting to be made. Eric backed away from the mirror.

"No," he said aloud. But there was no one to hear it.

He felt the need for a shower. Cleanse. Start fresh. Mean it.

Chapter 19

But he knew how that went. He'd lived inside that loop his whole life.

This is how it starts.

Eric shook the shadow of Howard off him and dragged himself to the kitchen. The faucet ran cold only. The heat was cut three months ago. He gulped. Water spilled onto his shirt, over his mouth, mixing with tears already wetting his face.

How you doin', kiddo?

Eric's stomach lurched. *Not great.*

He made it to the toilet just in time to lift both lids and projectile vomit bluish liquor, staining the porcelain bowl. After a few hours moaning and groaning on the cool hard tile, Eric blinked his eyes sober and got to his feet.

He flipped a light switch. His old bedroom filled with posters of swimsuit models and Wayne Gretzky looked like a set from a TV show. Unlived in. Fake. His bed was still made, though the cowboys had ridden off to storage making room for his dad's old quilt.

Eric ran his fingers along the expert stitching and tactile handiwork of his grandmother. Various colors, different patches, all sewn together to highlight and surround one word: *Gelassenheit.*

Surrender.

Eric was far from the Mennonite religion that had shunned his father. Surrendering to God, for Howard, meant taking his own life.

Dad found Gelassenheit his own way.

Eric thought about his mom. About Tanya. About all the women he'd been with then left.

Maybe I should too.

He pressed his face into the carpet and sobbed the way he hadn't since Joanne died thirteen weeks and four days ago. Not that he'd been intentionally counting. His shattered heart had been keeping its own calendar like the discordant metronome it was.

"I don't want to be like my dad!" he cried.

He thought of Howard. His promises that cleared the air for a night, then funked up the place by morning. All the women his dad hurt and lied to, including his mom.

"I can't do this anymore," Eric told the ceiling. "Please. I can't do this." He collapsed onto the quilt, grasping it in muscular-yet-weak hands. "I surrender. I surrender! *Gelassenheit!*"

The weight slowly loosened as he handed over his grief, anger, and addictions to sex and booze. That night, Eric slept on his childhood bed without nightmares, worry, or the haunting sounds of a drunk, woman-chasing dad.

The next morning, he went back to the house he owned and told Tanya he was done. She rolled her eyes when he mentioned his surrender to God. She threw a shoe as she told him he was replacing one addiction with another. She said he was a loser as she drove away from his house for the very last time. He sold his and his mom's house for more than both of their asking price. He packed up and left Elmira within a week. Once he settled into his new condo in downtown Toronto, Eric downloaded HerTrue and filled out the profile carefully.

Maybe that prince from his bedtime story didn't have to be make-believe after all.

20

After five days and four sleepless nights spent glued to her laptop, Dee came up empty-handed. Police, banks, and credit card companies all hit dead ends. Madison Wheelock, a.k.a. Madison Cotto, had cleaned out her apartment, sold her Kia, adopted another new name, and disappeared clean with the Taylors' money.

Eric trod carefully around his wife. Dee was mean, cold, and cutting. He moved quiet like a dormouse, cautious not to ask questions he already knew the answers to. He didn't want to add to any more of Dee's stress.

After cops, agents, bankers, and Eric confirmed the low probability of finding Madison, Dee gave up her search. On the floor of her closet, she unzipped another garment bag. This one contained a navy Versace suit. Dee reached inside the sleeve. Her eyes landed on the dress's price tag. Her stomach churned.

Next to her, Eric leaned over her shoulder. "Five thousand, nine hundred," he murmured, writing the number in a ledger.

Dee flinched. She straightened and shifted position.

He tallied the designer shirts, pants, suits, and dresses: $237,950 spent on 76 items.

"This is good news. We can fix this." Eric placed his hand on Dee's thigh reassuringly.

Dee rose to her feet, shunning his touch as if he were one of the overpriced items that disgusted her.

Earlier, Eric had offered to sell his campervan and power tools to sweeten the pot.

"Absolutely not!" Dee said.

He tried to argue and debate. They were in this together. But Dee insisted he not sell anything of his own. She barely convinced him she wanted to sell her entire couture collection. Luckily, everything still had tags; otherwise, he wouldn't have believed her. The bright spot was that Dee was finally getting rid of the clothes.

Eric pushed himself off the floor. Dee admired his athleticism. Watching him stretch, a wave of attraction washed over her. Despite the apathy, he was all hers. But, just like the clothes, there were no returns. She allowed her eyes to linger on his perky rear.

"Are you checking out my bum?" Eric asked with a hint of appreciation.

"I—" Dee stumbled, caught. She ate the lie she'd almost told. "Yes. I love your butt."

"Ooh, baby." Eric wiggled his behind at her.

Dee laughed and grabbed two fistfuls of his taut ass. She threw her arms around him, surprising them both.

"Thanks for helping me through this. I couldn't do it alone."

"Yeah, right." Eric wrapped his strong arms around her. "You do everything alone. But I'm here for you. Happy to help."

Dee wrapped herself in his embrace. She lifted her chin. Eye to eye. Nose to nose. Eric leaned in first. Dee met him halfway. Their kiss was conscientious. Her body warmed fast. Eric's hands slid over her hips.

Beep beep beep.

Dee tore off her watch and flung it to the floor. Her hands went to the zipper of his jeans.

Eric paused. "Are you sure?"

Chapter 20

Dee bobbed her head. The time was now or else it would stay never.

They moved toward the bed. The mattress dipped under their weight. His hands were gentle, slow. She pulled him closer, impatient.

Hurry up, she mentally urged him. There was definitely no foreplay.

When he pushed into her, pain came fast. She stiffened, legs locked together.

Eric felt it. "Dee—"

"I'm fine. Keep going."

Dee willed herself on. Eric thrust inside her again. She pushed him off hard.

"Stop!" The word came out harsh. She tried to soften. "I can't. It hurts."

Eric immediately pulled back. "You okay?"

She sat up, heart racing. "My stupid body..."

"There's nothing stupid about you," he said, reaching for her arm.

She stood before his fingers could find her. She grabbed her clothes and pulled them on fast. Eric dressed slower. The bed between them was rumpled and unfinished. Neither knew what to say next, so they didn't say anything. Dee's body already said enough.

21

Dee inhaled and exhaled through her nose, settling into her long run. She ran without earbuds, listening to her breath and the steady slap of sneakers on pavement. The rhythm soothed her. As the grey dawn sky gave way to the pink and orange hues of sunrise, Dee tried to shed the weight from the past week. Her efforts failed.

"He must be furious," Dee said aloud. "I know I would be."

Eric mumbled "good night" and went to sleep. Dee didn't ask how he felt about everything. She wasn't sure she cared.

Her stride lengthened. She was barely five miles in and already winded. She shifted her thoughts from problems to solutions. Like LuxCon, the site where she'd resell all her name-brand items and recoup her money. After Eric started snoring, Dee pulled out her old camera and lighting kit. When Run Café was thriving, she filmed constantly — races, tips, community events. The website hadn't been updated in years.

She moved fast and methodically, adjusting lights, framing shots, changing outfits. The clothes photographed well. So did Dee. She would sell everything. She knew it.

Dee stood in front of the camera, twirling, twisting, measuring, and modeling each item. She found an effortless rhythm. Five hours later, she documented every overpriced piece of her closet in an online auction. All she needed to do was craft the write-ups, upload the photos and videos, and she could release her financial guilt to the wind.

Dee inhaled the fresh Kentucky air as she settled into mile six of twelve.

One thing down, seven thousand to go.

22

The smell of pancakes hit her before she reached the kitchen. Eric stood at the stove, his back to her, waving his culinary white flag in surrender. But something in his posture was careful and deliberate. Like he'd been rehearsing for this moment all morning.

As she stepped further into her home, Eric set a plate of syrupy pancakes topped with bananas at her usual stool at the island. Their conversation skimmed the surface. Dee's run. Breakfast. The weather. Both had more to say and didn't.

He hates me, she thought.

Dee lifted the final bite, ready to start a real conversation. Her phone interrupted, vibrating on the counter. Shaking syrup onto the empty plate.

Buzzzzz buzzzzz buzzzzzz.

Eric nudged the phone toward her. "Same number a few times while you were out."

Rather than risk awkward silence or confront her feelings, she answered.

"Hello?"

"This Dee Moreland?" a harried country voice asked.

"Yes." Though who was calling Dee by her maiden name was unknown.

Chapter 22

"This is Candy Williams with Empowered Gifts in Lexington. We spoke before." Dee's stomach dropped. She knew who this was. "I'll cut to it, Miss Moreland. Eighty women arrived this morning, so we had to change our policy. We'll take everything you've got now. Luxury items, brand names. Whatever. These women need clothes bad."

Months ago, Dee talked to Candy, begging for flexibility. Now Dee needed cash.

Say it's gone, a frantic voice inside Dee urged.

She opened her mouth to lie. Eric watched her, reading the strain in her face. He reached across the island and touched her hand. Dee met his eyes. She knew what he would do. She also knew what he would say. A calmer voice rose inside her.

Donate everything.

It was unmistakable. Gentle instruction. Before she could hesitate, Dee clutched the phone and closed her eyes.

"When can you come pick everything up?"

23

______

Dee taped the final box shut. Except for whatever lingered in the trash, she had cleared away all the contents from her Run Café. Eric watched her press the last strip of duct tape on the cardboard so the top wouldn't come apart like she was.

In a moment of unexpected generosity, Dee decided not to just donate all her luxury items to Empowered Gifts, but she also threw in a down winter coat, a beloved wool blazer, a pair of Frye boots, and a form-fitting cashmere sweater Eric regretted seeing go. Eighty items total. Not a single tear shed. Eric watched on in silent admiration.

"That's it," Dee said, patting the box. "Run Café is officially closed."

"For now," Eric added, lifting the box. "It's on pause, not stop."

The bell above the door tinkled as he carried the final box outside. Dee exhaled. Twenty years trying to build a running community and she didn't have a dollar or a friend to show for it.

"What's next?" Dee directed the question at the empty café and all that lay above it.

The bell chimed as Eric returned. "We're locked and loaded. Ready to go?"

Chapter 23

Dee gritted her teeth. His cheerfulness scraped against her last nerve. She searched for an excuse to run the four miles home. Anything to avoid sitting beside his unwelcome optimism. But no excuse made sense.

"I'll meet you in the car. I'm gonna sweep up," Dee said through clenched teeth. She needed a buffer before sharing more space with him.

"No problem, sweetheart." Eric knew giving her space meant her breaking down and hugging the walls in teary farewell.

The bell tinkled as he exited Run Café the final time. Dee's eyes stung at the sound. She remembered Eric walking into her shop years ago, wide-eyed and dazzled. Then, the café had been empty, barren of people, products, and love. To Eric, she was a small business owner following her passion. He didn't notice the dust on expired protein bars or the lack of foot traffic. He only saw the dream she breathed into life. A trait Dee both loved and envied in him, but now couldn't stand.

Alone and empty, the café felt larger than ever. Memories of the past twenty-odd years flooded her. Run Café was her sanctuary. Closing its doors allowed grief to return with the same sharp edge she was cut with when her family died. Similar questions followed.

What now? What next?

Tears fell. Dee slid to the floor. A heavy sandbag of despair. She sobbed until sadness mutated into rage. Dee's fists tightened, making contact with her temples. She searched for something to smash aside from her face. Only a broom, dustpan, and trash can remained.

"How could I have been so stupid?" Her voice rose, directed at the ceiling. "Why are you doing this to me? I can't take it anymore!"

She kicked the trash like she was scoring a goal, scattering junk mail across the floor.

"HELP ME!"

Dee picked up mail and flung it back across the room. She

imagined the letters and flyers turned to bricks that would demolish the café's walls. Envelopes thudded unsatisfactorily. Papers drifted like feathers. Most everything fell softer than she hoped. One glossy flyer, however, pirouetted midair, spun inward, and landed at the tip of her sneaker. Dee bent down, curious.

"What do you want?" she asked it.

Her eyes widened as she read about the Blue Ridge Mountain 100K ultramarathon, then rolled at the sexist prize split.

"No way."

The calm voice inside whispered:

Do this together.

Dee cocked her head, questioning. She reread the flyer. It'd be a $35,000 prize if a man and woman won together.

"You cannot be telling me to run an ultramarathon with Eric. He doesn't run." Dee doubted the voice and her sanity. "And the end of October's only a few months away."

You can win.

Dee didn't know if the thought came from her own mind or elsewhere. Either way, scripture followed.

Trust in the Lord with all your heart and lean not on your own understanding; in all your ways submit to Him, and He will make your paths straight.

"This is crazy," she said, trying to dismiss the flyer as dumb luck.

But earlier disobedience nagged at her: Spending money unwisely. Saying yes to sex when she knew she wasn't ready. Keeping the café open. She was surrounded by the wreckage of all her poor decisions.

Wanna keep repeating the same mistakes?

She weighed the flyer. Victory would put them in the black. Working together would bring them closer. Gift. Chance. Opportunity. She asked and here was the answer.

Eric hates to run, she argued.

The voice replied.

But he loves you.

24

___

Eric sat brooding in the van. He considered going back inside to see what was taking so long. Then Dee burst out of the café grinning.

"I got it!" she shouted, waving the flyer.

"What'd you get?"

Dee ran to his door as he opened it. "We're gonna win an ultramarathon!" She thrust the flyer at him. Eric took it and read.

"I love you, but no. I don't run."

Dee's smile only widened. "Hockey is nothing but a run on ice."

"It's more than that."

Dee rubbed his arm the same way he'd stroked hers the night before. "Please?"

"It's impossible. This race is less than seven months away!"

"You can do it! I believe in you." Dee beamed, shoving his own toxic positivity back at him. A prick of guilt nipped at her, but she pressed further. "You won't even have to run the whole way. You can walk a lot of it," she lied.

Eric stared, hearing but not listening. He imagined the distance from Toronto to Buffalo. Eric loved Dee, but running? Never.

"Dee..." He plopped back into his driver's seat.

"Eric," she cooed flirtatiously. Her honeyed voice dripped as she pressed the flyer back into his limp hand. "This literally fell at my feet. If we train together, we can win."

Eric melted like grilled cheese. He'd longed to hear her say "together" without her usual question of "if they should be" tacked on.

"It'll be good for our marriage," Dee added.

"You think our marriage is bad?"

"No," she said, stroking his arm. "But this will help."

Eric sighed and handed her the flyer back.

"What do I have to do?"

25

Dee had big plans for her giant dry-erase board when it was first delivered to Run Café. Each morning, with her impeccable handwriting, she filled the board with the day's temperature, chance of rain, sunrise and sunset times, plus a Run Café quote. The whiteboard became her customers' inspirational touchstone. It gave her so much joy.

Which was why Eric's groan stung so much as she wheeled it into the living room for his first lesson.

"Come on, I'm watching that," he whined as Dee muted the hockey game.

"Running is more than just feet on the ground," Dee said, ignoring his protest. "There's a science to it. Especially if you want to win."

She wrote *ANAEROBIC* and *AEROBIC* on the board.

"Can't you wait for the game to end?" Eric craned his neck to watch the TV behind her.

"We only have half a year to completely retrain your hockey body." Eric sat transfixed by the screen. "And your hockey brain." Dee turned off the TV.

"Dee!"

She cocked her head with a look that said, *Stop it*, so he did.

"Hockey is an anaerobic sport," Dee said, underlining the word. "Hockey players need quick energy for sprints, speed, and shots. Hockey defines high-intensity exercise."

Eric perked up. She was speaking his language. He leaned back on the sofa, cocky. "Ain't that the truth."

Dee closed her eyes so she wouldn't roll them. "Long-distance running is aerobic." She tapped the word with her marker. "Runners train in a zone that doesn't build high lactate levels."

"Got it," Eric said, not understanding at all.

"To condition you as a runner, we need to find your comfortable running pace that keeps your heart rate low."

"Walking is my comfortable pace."

"No walking. You might finish the race, but you won't win."

"You said I could walk!"

"Not the whole time!"

"I'd never have agreed to this if—"

"This will make you a better hockey player."

Eric stopped. She hit his weak spot. "Fine. So now what?"

"Wear this." Dee pulled an older Garmin from her pocket and tossed it to Eric. As soon as he put it on—

Beep beep beep.

The watch blared the same alarm Dee's did when her heart rate jolted. She lifted an eyebrow. "Gimme that."

Eric handed over her watch. Dee examined it quizzically. Nothing should have triggered the alarm. She'd cleared her own data while prepping for the first lesson with Eric. She maxed the Garmin at 200 BPM, an absurdly high heart rate for endurance running. She knew his heart rate shouldn't be anywhere near that high. No healthy person would hit 200 BPM except — according to the Garmin — Eric.

Dee triple-checked the watch, then eyed her husband nervously. "You're not having a heart attack, are you?"

"What? No!"

Chapter 25

Dee sat beside him. She grabbed his wrist and checked his pulse with two fingers. "Then why is your heart rate over two-hundred beats per minute?"

Eric squirmed. "It does that sometimes. It's normal."

"Normal? How?"

"I've had it since I was a kid. It's—"

"Tachycardia?"

"Yeah. That."

"Why didn't you tell me?!" Dee scowled, her eyes soft with worry.

Eric never thought of it. He was fine. He limited coffee. Exercised. Stayed healthy. It was genetic from his mom.

"Would you have married me if you knew I had a heart arrhythmia?"

"Of course." Dee scooted closer. "Does the school know?"

Eric played hockey as hard as the teens he coached. He knew the risks. He adapted when flutters struck. But he didn't tell anyone.

"No," he admitted.

Dee squeezed his wrist, not to check his pulse, but to comfort him. "I don't want you playing hockey anymore." Eric met her eyes. "I don't want you running either."

"But—"

"No buts."

"Dee..."

She raised her hand. No discussion. She was done with death. She couldn't lose Eric too. "Maybe the school will let you coach without playing."

"We need the income," Eric said, not thinking. True, yes, but incredibly harsh.

Dee stared at him, catching the sting of rejection. She could be a tiger when mad. He braced for the roar.

"I'll find a job soon," she snapped, then stood and left the room.

Eric called after her but knew it was useless. She wouldn't return until she calmed down. He knew chasing would only spark a fight. He didn't have to strain to hear Dee slamming kitchen cabinets. He decided to give her time to cool down. Because of his heart, the plan was over before it started. He picked up the remote and tuned back to hockey. Still on mute, to be safe.

26

———

Dee sat at the dinner table, moping and pushing mushy whatever it was around on her plate. Eric choked down his meal with water and extra salt.

"Thanks for dinner," he said, trying to eat her mess. "You forgive me for not telling you about my heart?"

Dee flicked her eyes to his as a warning while cutting a piece of soggy nutritional yeast-topped tofu with her fork.

"I'm not upset about that."

Eric gulped down a stalk of over-steamed cauliflower. "What are you upset about then?" He grabbed the saltshaker and dumped another heap on his oversaturated meal.

Dee snatched the shaker away. "This! You shouldn't even use this." She slouched in her chair. "How could you not tell me?"

She sounded wounded and sad. Her eyes grew wet. Her lower lip pooched. Eric jumped from his seat and wrapped his arms around her tightly.

"You're right. I'm sorry. I should've told you." Her tears soaked his sleeve with big, heavy drops. Eric held her closer. "I promise you I'm okay. My doctor said it's good for me to exercise. I need to use my heart, just not overdo it. But I won't eat salt and I won't play hockey if you don't want me to."

Dee sniffled. She lifted her head and looked him square in the eye. "I want you to go to the doctor. Here. In the U.S."

"Okay."

"And I want you to tell the school about your heart. If anything happened to you..." Dee laid her head on his shoulder, clutching him tight.

"Nothing's gonna happen. But fine, I'll tell them."

Dee curled into his arms. The possibility of losing Eric made her miss him in ways she didn't know were possible. All other worries disappeared. Only Eric mattered. She needed him. He always supported her. Always stayed positive. He loved her unconditionally.

Maybe that's why I push him away. I'm glad I found out before that stupid ultra.

As if he could read her mind: "I could still run that race."

"Absolutely not. I don't want you running. Ever. I can win by myself."

Dee pulled the older Garmin from her pocket and strapped it to Eric's left wrist. "Wear this from now on. Always. Hear me? It's set at two-hundred BPM. If the alarm goes off, stop whatever you're doing, lie down, and close your eyes."

"What if I'm driving?" Eric joked.

Dee was not having it. She repeated herself. "If the alarm goes off, stop and lie down."

"What should I do lying down?" He grinned like a doof.

Dee fumed. This was no laughing matter. She grabbed Eric's collar, balling it in her fist. "Pray."

She let go of him, leaving a wrinkled sign of her fury on his shirt.

Despite Dee's nagging, her concern made him smile wide.

"Stop grinning at me like that."

"You're worried about me," Eric teased.

"What if I am?" Dee folded her arms.

"You love me," Eric said sing-songy, leaning close.

Chapter 26

"Stop it." She pushed him away, barely.

"You love me," he repeated, inching closer to her mouth.

"Whatever." Dee allowed him into her personal space. Her lips puckered. Instantly, Eric's mouth was on hers.

Neither of their watches sounded the alarm.

27

———

Dee sat on the lone chair in the exam room, clutching her phone tight against her knees. Eric dangled his socked feet from the examining table, whistling the song they heard in the waiting room: Rick Astley's "Never Gonna Give You Up." She despised its apropos lyrics.

Death is a giant Rickroll from the sky.

For two days, Eric wore a Holter monitor. His EKG returned normal. Now, after spending hours as a pincushion with a batch of catheters in his veins, Dee and Eric awaited the results from his electrophysiology study.

Dee clenched her fists, nails biting into her palms. She fought against prayer and scripture, but her anxious mind defaulted.

If this is a test, I don't know if I can pass it.

Dee tumbled toward doubt. She was about to blow. Hours passed. Finally, the exam-room door opened. Dee's sharp nails moved from her indented fists to the tops of her jeans. Dr. Jones stepped inside. Eric waved at the doctor like a child.

"What's up, doc?"

Dee closed her eyes, restraining herself from lashing out at her husband for treating a serious moment so lightly.

"Well, you have Paroxysmal Supraventricular Tachycardia,"

Dr. Jones said, shutting the door behind him. He peeked over the top of his reading glasses and smiled kindly at Eric. Then he turned his gaze to Dee. "Don't worry. Your husband is fine."

Dee exhaled as her shoulders dropped from around her ears.

"I'm sorry about Run Café," Jones added. "I always encouraged my patients to visit. It's all our loss."

Dr. Leroy Jones was Greenup's only cardiologist. He'd been an early supporter of Run Café. Someone Dee trusted for years.

Jones turned to Eric. "You play hockey." His tone was matter of fact.

"Yessir," Eric said, waggling his stocking feet.

"Eric tells me you want him to run an ultramarathon," Jones said to Dee.

Dee felt a surge of guilt. "Not anymore!" She didn't want Dr. Jones thinking she'd tried to kill her husband. That kind of drama belonged in Lifetime movies, not Greenup. "That was before I knew about his heart."

Jones scanned his notes on his clipboard while humming "Never Gonna Give You Up." Eric swayed his shoeless feet.

"I think it's a good idea," Jones finally said, nodding approval at his own opinion. "Endurance running will be good for you," he told Eric. "It'll strengthen your heart."

Dee's jaw dropped. "What?!"

"He needs a doctor's recommendation, right? Now he has it. Let him run." Jones clapped his hand on Eric's back.

Eric smiled wide. If the doctor Dee trusted so much gave his thumbs-up, Dee could finally stop worrying. Or at least she *should*. But Eric could tell by the look on Dee's face she hadn't stopped agonizing. Her brows cemented into a V for volatile. Even when Dee slept, she looked unsettled, her brows forever locked into that familiar V. Eric watched it form even in rest. But he couldn't say anything to calm her. Worry and doubt were synonymous with Dee.

"You're saying that with Eric's heart that sometimes spikes

over *two-hundred beats per minute*, he's cleared to run a sixty-mile race?"

"Yes." Jones smiled. "I am." Eric's legs swung with delight.

Dee sputtered. "How?"

Dee didn't trust Dr. Jones like her husband did. Her trust in him cracked.

Jones laughed. "He's not going to up and run it tomorrow, Dee. He must train. You know that better than anyone."

She understood how training could strengthen a heart. And how it could destroy one. "You're crazy! You're both nuts!"

"Maybe," Jones said, patting Eric on the back again. "But I think Eric would make a fine runner. Just don't overdo it. Stay in your heart's comfort zone. If you feel dizzy, stop."

"And pray," Eric added, recalling Dee's advice.

Dee's eyes cut to Eric. "I can't believe you're joking about this."

Dr. Jones rolled up his sleeve and revealed his watch. "If you're that concerned, I recommend you get Eric a watch like this and track his heart rate through the app. That way, you know how he's doing in real time."

"That's the one Dee gave me!"

"Good. Use it." Jones leaned toward Eric, demonstrating the Garmin's functions. "You can set it to alert you when you hit your target heart rate as well as your threshold. That's how you'll find your sweet spot."

"Nice!"

Dee watched the two men fawn over the gadget with disbelief. She just endured an emotional gauntlet to avoid losing her husband. Now she had to figure out how to train Eric without killing him.

And this is doctor's orders?!

She racked her brain while making a follow-up appointment with reception. Dee desperately needed positive news. Maybe Eric's thumbs-up was it.

"Your wife is understandably upset," Dr. Jones said to Eric

as he walked him out. "Remember, 'it's better to live on the roof of your house than with a wife who always argues.'" He winked.

Eric followed Dee down the hall. She didn't look at him. Dr. Jones' proverb hung in the air between them like smoke. The warning dressed as wisdom, Eric stayed mute.

Dee jabbed the elevator button. The doors opened. Inside, she stared straight ahead, her brow locked in a furrow she couldn't release. Eric stood beside her, quiet. She waited for him to say something. A question. A plea. A negotiation. But he said nothing. She didn't know if that was better or worse.

Eric's right, Dee thought. *Walking might be safest.*

The elevator hummed.

Hockey is violent. Sprints. Explosions. Survival. That's all heart.

Their bodies jostled as they lowered to the ground floor.

Endurance is different. Pacing. Breath. Control.

Dee and Eric stood side by side, each ready to give something up for the other, unsure yet of the cost.

Isn't there another exercise he can use to cross-train without blowing up his heart?

The elevator stopped at the ground floor. Doors dinged open. Eric let Dee exit first, but she stopped cold when she was suddenly face-to-face with her OBGYN, Dr. Bruder.

Try foreplay.

"Hello, Mrs. Taylor," Bruder said. Her voice was like squeaky helium slowly released from a balloon. "Is this your husband?"

Dee's Garmin blared as her heart rate spiked. She reset it instead of speaking.

Eric stuck out his hand. "Yeah, hi. I'm Eric."

I hate this evil woman more than anyone in the world, Dee thought.

"Let's let these people get on their way, sweetheart," Eric said, moving Dee aside.

"Bye," Bruder said as the elevator doors closed.

Dee's eyes bored holes through the metal, willing her gynecologist to disintegrate like her own self-confidence that Bruder had shredded.

From inside her heart, the echo of her doctor's words spun.

Try foreplay.

Outside in the parking lot, warm April sun kissed Dee's skin. She closed her eyes, counting to ten. Dee's watch alarm went off again. She pressed reset.

Eric pointed to the elevator. "Who was that?"

"My gynecologist."

Eric let the comment go. If Dee wanted to elaborate, she would.

First, I have to worry about cross-training my dumb husband without killing him. Now my awful gyno reminds me of my failures as a wife? What kind of cruel torture—

TRY FOREPLAY!

Dee's eyes popped open.

"Oh!" She gasped, then flushed, then chuckled. No longer enraged.

Eric looked around. "What's funny?"

"Come on," Dee barked, marching to her car. Her emotions climbed back up the roller-coaster track.

Sweat beaded across Eric's temples as he chased after her.

I hate running, he thought but didn't say, heeding Dr. Jones' sage advice.

28

Dee waited until Eric's footsteps faded down the hall and out the front door. She listened for the growl of his van, then the scrape of balding tires on stone. When all sounds disappeared, she counted to thirty, marking each second with an *alligator*. Only then did she pull the curtains closed, room by room.

At the bottom drawer, beneath technical race shirts and forgotten medals, lay a purple velvet bag and a small white box. She carried both to the bathroom, turned on the light, and ran the warm water. First, she opened the velvet sack. Inside was something that looked like a giant silicone crazy straw, but wasn't. A pelvic floor wand was far less fun.

She washed the wand under the tap, embarrassed to hold it, even while alone. This wasn't a sex toy, it was rehab. She pressed the power button by accident and the wand roared to life, vibrating violently, spraying water across the sink and tile. Dee yelped, fumbled, and eventually shut it off. Heart racing, she laid it on a towel. Dust clung to the bag. It cost a fortune. Understandably, something that goes inside your vagina cannot be refunded.

Next was the white box that held eight silicone dilators, each a different size and color. The smallest looked apologetic. The largest punitive. Hot pink Number Eight was out of the question. Like the Goldilocks of menopause, Dee chose blue Number Six and washed it. Beneath suds and soap, it felt tolerable. Not good but hopefully just right.

Back in the bedroom, she stripped from the waist down and slid under the sheets. From her nightstand, she pulled out lube, vaginal estrogen, and a prescription tube of vaginal lidocaine with her name printed on the side. She mixed them together in her palms and coated the wand and dilator until slick. This was the unsexy work required to avoid excruciating sex.

She exhaled, bent her knees, inserted the wand just shallow enough not to hurt, and turned it on. The default vibration felt weak. Dee scrolled through modes until she found the strongest one. She set a fifteen-minute timer on her Garmin and guided the wand like a video-game controller, working tissue that hadn't been touched in years.

She had only used this stuff once, long before Eric. She'd still been a virgin when Dr. Bruder first sent her to pelvic floor therapy. Only a small cytobrush had ever seen her insides. No speculum. No tampons. Bruder warned Dee she needed elasticity and moisture, stat.

Pelvic floor therapy was worse than the pap smear. When the therapist suggested a manual exam, Dee froze.

"Use your hand where?"

She feared bleeding. Pain. Ruin. In her mid-thirties, nothing ever entered her — not a penis or even a finger. Only pads. Only control. Virginity wasn't a virtue so much as an unpickable lock. Church taught Dee that her body was borrowed. Blood made it unclean. Desire made it dangerous. Leviticus handled the rest. No one challenged it. Staying sealed was how Dee learned to be good.

Now, medicine said the opposite. Flex or tear. Stretch or bleed. Christianity demanded purity. Her body wanted circulation. Eventually, biology won. The therapist explained it simply: use it or lose it. The assessment hurt. The diagnosis was brutal.

Chapter 28

Thin tissue. Inflammation. Atrophy. If Dee wanted her body to change, she needed to take it to the gym.

The wand shut off automatically. She switched to the dilator, lubing herself numb, breathing through the stretch, easing Six into place. Bigger was the goal. Someday. Not yet.

She bought the tools but never opened the box. Until now, she didn't need them.

Back then, she didn't know about Eric's heart.

His heart rate didn't spike when we kissed. If it can handle sex, it can handle training, she thought. *I can strengthen him myself.*

She reset her watch for another fifteen minutes. She didn't imagine or picture any sexual activity, only the closeness afterward. The part that came with breathing together. The part that felt safe.

Too bad I have to go through penetration to get there.

She pulled *The Seven Levels of Intimacy* from her nightstand drawer. With the dilator releasing tension between her thighs, Dee lay back and opened the book to "Level Four: Hopes & Dreams."

For Dee, sex wasn't intimacy. It was conditioning. And she was its coach.

29

By the time Eric got home, Dee had washed, dried, and packed everything back into the drawer.

Some things people don't need to share, she told herself.

"Dee?" Eric called as he stepped inside, half-expecting, half-wishing she'd come running. They both carried a Disney-esque fairy-tale version of marriage in their heads, even if their reality leaned closer to the Brothers Grimm.

Dee hovered in the kitchen, scanning a Kroger circular she'd grabbed at random. Eric noticed she didn't greet him. He cleared his throat.

"Oh, hey," Dee said, looking up. "Didn't hear you come in."

She had never clipped a coupon a day in her life. She braced herself, certain he'd call her out for looking at them now. Eric didn't. He only noticed the chill in the room.

"What are you doing?" he asked.

"What does it look like?"

Abort, Eric told himself. *Compliment.* "You look nice."

"Thanks."

She wore light-gray sweatpants and prayed no cream or lubricant betrayed her and was staining her seat.

Eric opened the fridge. "Can I have this? It's the last banana."

Chapter 29

"I'll get more tomorrow," Dee said, noting a sale on bananas, committing fully to the lie.

He peeled it and watched her out of the corner of his eye. She felt secretive, short, and strange. They needed to talk about his heart, the race, and whatever came next. But the silence pressed on.

"I want to run," Eric said.

"Do you still want to run?" Dee said at the same time.

They laughed.

"Yes," Eric said, sitting across from her. "Do you still want to train me?"

"Yes," Dee said, too quickly. Inside, she thrilled. Purpose. Partnership. A plan.

Prayer.

She swatted that P away.

"Wanna start tonight?" she asked. She almost said, *I'm training for you*. Instead, she folded the circular.

"Sure," Eric said, ignoring the nausea curling in his stomach.

Why am I agreeing to this? he wondered, already knowing the answer.

Love.

30

———

Dee strapped the heart monitor around Eric's torso. His skin grew goosebumps under her fingers. She didn't notice. She was already syncing the monitor to both their Garmins, watching the numbers populate in real time. She wanted him aerobic. Slow. Conversation pace. Nose breathing. A heart rate that hovered, not spiked.

We'll get there, she told herself. *First, I need to see how he moves.*

Her eyes dropped to his sneakers. Ragged, sunken, wrong. He needed real running shoes. Orthotics. Technical socks. Gear they didn't own and couldn't afford. Running pretended to be simple, but it was a rich person's sport. Roads were free. Everything else cost.

If he wins, it's worth it, she thought. *All of it.*

"Run around the house and back," Dee said.

Eric took off, heart rate already climbing as he stretched. One minute in, he was at 170. Dee frowned. Moments later, Eric came back red-faced, sweat pouring, breath heaving.

"Done."

Dee checked her watch. Under two minutes. "You ran the whole property?"

Chapter 30

Eric gulped air and traced a small circle with his finger. "House."

Dee sighed and put a hand on his back. His heart rate dropped instantly, another data point she did not notice. "I meant all the way around. It's just under a mile."

He shook his head and collapsed. When he was done, he meant it.

Dee handed him water. "You're running like it's hockey. Fast and explosive isn't endurance." She watched sweat pour off him. The monitor didn't short-circuit, though she expected it to. "Get up," she said, tugging his sleeve.

Eric sat, sucking her thermos like an infant. How he played hockey baffled her. Though she'd never seen him play. Never once gone to a game. The guilt wanted to stay. She pushed past it quick.

"No sitting," Dee said, pulling him to his feet. "I'm pacing you." She jogged ahead of him, so slow it barely qualified. Eric shuffled to keep up.

"I can walk faster than this," he said.

"Then walk," she replied. "Nose breathing only."

He tried. Failed. His heart rate climbed anyway. "I can't," he said, stopping.

Dee checked her watch: 180. They hadn't even cleared the driveway.

"Okay," she said, recalibrating. "New plan. One-minute run. One-minute walk." Interval training. Beginner-proof. Even ultra-runners used it.

They took off again. Eric watched her body move. Hips steady, effortless. He forgot himself and zoned in on his wife's form.

"Stop staring at my ass and run!"

He groaned and followed. Her watch buzzed. Time to walk.

"A walk break isn't rest," Dee said. "Hydrate. Roll your shoulders. Stay present."

Eric rolled his arms exaggeratedly. She didn't look up. She was busy checking his numbers: 157. She blinked.

Improvement!

"How do you feel?" she asked.

"Fine."

That was enough. They moved again. Run, walk, run. The orchard passed in vibrant bursts. Peach, apple, pear. Eric breathed it in, surprised by how calm it felt.

"There," Dee said softly. "That's the pace."

He glanced at her. She was smiling.

She likes this, he realized. *I might too.*

The watch buzzed. Walk.

"How often do I have to train?" he asked.

Dee was thinking ahead to gear. Schedules. Money. Two bodies that needed their own conditioning to survive what was being asked of them.

"More than you want," she said. *More than I want*, she thought.

She exhaled through her mouth.

I'll have to get myself ready sooner than I thought.

31

Interval training dropped Eric's heart rate from 170 to 140. Dee clocked the number with joy. Eric only felt the suffering. Every time Dee's watch buzzed at the end of a walk interval, Eric groaned, rolled his eyes, or muttered something under his breath. He didn't hate walking, but Dee needed him to love running if he was going to win. It was clear he hated every minute. Or at least every other minute. It was going to be a long road ahead.

After the workout, Eric headed straight for the bathroom, announcing plans for a long, hot shower. He shivered even though the air wasn't cold.

"Your temperature dropped," Dee said. "That's why you're freezing."

Eric didn't care about physiology. He smelled like sweat and failure and wanted both off him. Dee followed him partway, explaining lactic acid and recovery — topics she hadn't had anyone to discuss with in years.

She was grateful for Eric's long showers. He stayed under the water forever. She needed that. She needed space. She needed time alone. Because while Eric was cold, Dee felt warm — *down there*.

Maybe it was arousal. Maybe it was triumph. She'd taken her husband from zero to a few very slow loops around the house without killing him. She felt capable again. Useful. Pride, power, and heat pooled together inside her. She tried not to think about it. But it was there: want.

When the shower finally roared to life, Dee retrieved the purple velvet bag from the bottom drawer and slid under the covers, naked from the waist down. She mixed her menopause cocktail in her palm and numbed herself. The wand slid in easily. She pressed the power button.

Nothing. She pressed it again.

Why isn't it vibrating?

She pulled it out, scanned it, shook the bag, then dumped its contents onto the bed. A short black charging cable landed in a sad coil.

It's not charged. She listened to the shower. *No time now.*

She swapped the purple bag for the white box and crawled back under the covers. Eight silicone penii stared back at her.

"Which one?" she whispered.

She'd already tried Number Six — the one closest to Eric, she thought. She never studied him that way. Sex, for her, had always been theoretical. Menopause made it feel optional. But now her body buzzed.

Use it or lose it.

Ambitious, she chose Day-Glo green Number Seven. She lubed it generously and eased it inside. It didn't slide in like Six. She pushed it inside anyway. It didn't go all the way in.

Practice makes perfect, she thought, setting her watch for fifteen minutes.

In the bathroom, steam fogged the mirror as Eric wrestled with the heart monitor. He hadn't stepped in the shower yet. Not until he could get the monitor off. But it wouldn't come off without pulling hair, skin, or something important.

"I need help," he yelled as he bounded from the bathroom to Dee's side on the bed.

Dee scooted over immediately, giving him space to sit. The

mattress bounced. Number Seven shifted dangerously inside her. Closing in on an explosive exit.

"YEEOW!" Eric yelped as Dee tried tugging the strap off while ripping chest hair.

She turned him away from her, hands shaking. "Sorry, I almost got it."

"What's all over your hands?"

"Lotion." The lie made her knee jerk. The box tipped over. Colorful dilators spilled across the floor.

Eric stared and leaned closer. "What are those?"

Dee lunged for the box, but the covers slipped, exposing her naked-from-the-waist-down body and the unmistakable green silicone dangling from inside her.

"What is *that?!*"

Dee pulled the dilator out and dropped it on the bed between them.

"Pelvic floor therapy," she said more defeated than embarrassed. "For menopause pain."

Eric didn't look at her. He looked at the dilator.

"It's so big."

"Is it?"

"How long have you been doing this?"

"Under a year," she lied.

Two times. Both today. Close enough.

"Does it help?"

"Yes."

Also close enough.

"What does it do?"

Dee gestured with her hands instead of finding her words.

"Does it hurt?"

"Not really." She showed him the creams. "These help."

He nodded like he understood. He didn't. His eyes drifted to huge Number Eight.

"Do you use *all* of them?"

"No. I can't." She held Seven in her palm.

"That's bigger than me."

"I knew it."

"You did?"

Dee nodded, proud. Eric laughed. Relief flooded them both.

"I'm glad it helps," he said.

This was the worst possible moment to feel desire, and yet heat surged through her.

"Wanna have sex?" she asked.

Eric blinked. "Right now?"

"Yes."

He gestured at Seven. "I can't compete with that guy."

She smiled. "You don't have to."

He kissed her softly. She lubed him up and guided him in.

"Slow," she said. He listened.

As he moved inside her, Dee clocked Eric's heart rate on her watch over his shoulder.

"What do you want?" he asked as he rocked his hips.

Dee stayed silent but thought:

I want you to win.

32

———

Kentucky spring collapsed into a humid Greenup summer. Flowers bloomed, trees wilted, and people fled to the Sandy River. By the Fourth of July, Eric and Dee had swapped baseball caps for thick headbands to keep sweat out of their eyes. Eric shook apples and peaches from their trees for baking once the house cooled enough for the oven. They ate eggs purchased from a neighbor's chickens and made salads with herbs from farmers markets, toasting their meals with chilled white wine.

By mid-July, they had perfected a system: long runs, short runs, and vigorous, heart-pounding sex. Eric loved the latter most — especially since he had no idea their lovemaking was being used for training. Endorphins sanded their lives smooth. Work felt easier. Problems loosened their grip. For the first time, the Taylor house felt light, functional, and almost happy.

Eric adapted to run-walk training faster than Dee expected. Six minutes running, one walking. Marathon pace: 8:43 per mile. Not yet race-ready, but close enough to trust the plan. Three months remained. Plenty of time.

Dee tracked his heart: 125 while running, 96 while walking, 170 while fornicating. She pushed him hard. They ditched the chest strap for Eric's Garmin, secretly synced to Dee's watch. Sex complicated her monitoring. She hurried Eric into bed before he could shower. Sometimes she made him put the watch back on immediately after a cold rinse. Skin clean, hair damp, just to capture the data.

The lidocaine dulled her vaginal canal and dulled everything else too. After dozens of sessions, Dee never once climaxed. She didn't know what an orgasm was supposed to feel like. A childhood without girlfriends plus a faith that labeled curiosity dangerous left her without language. Sex education was abstinence, period. Desire was theoretical and born of TV.

Eric treated her pleasure like a measure of effort. Each session became a test of endurance, intensity, and finish. He worked harder, longer, determined. He didn't know she was too numb to let go. She faked it well. He mistook her volume for satisfaction. The commands, the frequency, the urgency — all of it read as proof.

Still, Dee enjoyed herself. She liked to shout commands. *Faster. Harder. Go.* Eric's climaxes intensified. Hers never came. She watched him and steered him instead, preparing him for his first twenty-miler. Dee thought variety might help. They experimented with positions. She proved quite acrobatic. After one long, sweaty session, Eric came so loudly, a flock of bank swallows burst from a nearby tree, peppering the yard with droppings. His heart hit 190 in bed, but never once went above 128 on a brutal and hilly run later that same day.

The results thrilled her, though she couldn't tell him. He'd be horrified to know intimacy was strategy. Luckily, Eric stayed blissfully unaware. He loved Dee's sudden carnal hunger. It thrilled him. And Dee's theory held. Elite training, smoother marriage. Everything worked. Mostly.

Sometimes Eric hesitated when Dee announced, "Let's have sex," while he was washing dishes or watching hockey. He never refused. He just wanted seduction. But Dee never seduced. Sex was diagnostic. Top, bottom, side, inverted. She collected outcomes and numbers. Intimacy under a microscope.

While Eric worked, Dee trained herself, stretching, enduring, preparing her body for his determined thrusts. One time as he came, his heart rate dropped from 168 to 120. Dee soaked up the number with joy.

The couple that trains together stays together, she thought as he rolled off her.

She liked the structure, schedules, regimens, and control. Shaping her husband excited her. Sex aroused her — not erotically, but functionally. Utility felt righteous.

For the first time, scripture made sense. *The wife does not have authority over her own body.* Sex wasn't for pleasure but for purpose. To submit was to win the race, the marriage, even life itself. And she had running to thank for all of it.

Without eye contact, Dee talked as they ran, getting vulnerable. They discussed old trips and imagined futures. She opened in ways she hadn't in decades, if ever. Training stripped something loose. Intimacy Level Four had finally been obtained.

Eric found himself wanting more time with his wife, even if it meant time spent on a run. His friends teased him for leaving after games early.

"We're newlyweds," he said skipping out on locker-room beers. His teammates joked about ball-and-chains and fading honeymoons, missing the truth entirely.

One morning, Dee and Eric set out for his first taste of a marathon. A sticky twenty-six miles with air that clung like pea soup. To distract themselves, they talked about snow, then Christmas. Dee told a story of how one year, the Moreland tree caught fire. Morris fumbled the extinguisher, got foam everywhere, and precious ornaments melted into plastic puddles.

Eric shared the memory of his mom's pot roast. He even told his dad's cheesy jokes.

"Why'd Santa go to music school?"

"Oh no. Why?"

"To improve his *wrap* skills."

They learned through stories. They deepened their knowledge of each other — literally and carnally. Morning. Night. Sometimes two or three times a day. Things were going well.

But when Eric prayed, Dee seethed. When he went still, eyes closed, then returned, Dee had no access. That made her angry and distrusting. She doled out the rules for Eric's prayers.

"Don't talk about me."

Eric never asked Dee to pray with him. Sometimes that felt like mercy. Other times, it felt like exclusion.

If he asks, I'll say no.

She replaced faith with discipline. Schedules instead of belief. Control instead of submission. Still, God's name surfaced constantly. When she needed help. When Eric offered to run errands. When things went smoothly. When Eric spent time with Him instead of her.

Dee long abandoned Ephesians and defied Corinthians: *The head of the woman is the man.* She took scripture as random passing thoughts and nothing else.

Other than money, her life was good. She needed no head. And neither did Eric. At least that's what she told him.

Eric finished praying and opened his eyes. Dee sat above him, staring.

"You okay?" He rubbed her knee.

"Yeah." She let his hand stay.

In three months, she'd softened. This Dee — direct, tireless, insatiable — felt nothing like the woman he married. Not better. Just different.

Dee watched his hand on her leg and felt an easy satisfaction settle into place. If she didn't tell him what to do — how fast to run, how hard to go at her, when to stop — he wouldn't know what was required. Why he needed a second opinion through God was annoying, but she let it go. He'd already shared what he needed when they first met in Canada. And to Dee, knowing what was required was the same thing as intimacy.

To her, their relationship was healthy.

33

The sun rose over rolling hills and forested terrain as Dee and Eric rounded the bend of Seaton Road. They left before dawn for a 50K. Eric's first foray into ultramarathoning.

The road was empty. Greenuppers either slept, fled to Louisville for the State Fair, or hid from the humidity and storms forecasted for later that day. Eric felt calm. Confident. He woke to early-morning sex — a daily routine now as Greenup's days grew hotter. But this morning felt different. Dee always initiated. Eric always followed her lead. Still, when the alarm stirred them awake at five, he felt an urgency in her that startled him. She climbed on top without hesitation. No lidocaine. No lube. The memory was hotter than the weather. The run would be easy. He had plenty to disappear into to bide his time.

Dee ran beside him, equally zoned out, but more bewildered. Hours earlier, she woke shaken and surprisingly wet, her body buzzing, demanding something she didn't yet understand. She lay there waiting for the alarm, barely breathing. When it rang, she didn't think, she moved. No preparation. No creams. For the first time in her life, she came.

Now, miles into the run, Dee felt split open, raw and overstimulated. Something old and impatient surged through her.

Heart rates, schmart rates. She wanted sex. She liked it. She responded to it — finally. The release left her unmoored and hungry. She was already thinking about getting home for round two.

She flirted openly. She took Eric's hand and pressed it to her butt when he reached for his coffee. She sprawled naked on the bed while he dressed. She told him she wanted him without looking away. Eric didn't question it. Desire arrived, sudden and welcome. He had no idea about her first-ever orgasm. He thought there had been many but there was only the one.

They huffed through miles seven and eight. The sky darkened overhead. The forecast promised storms later in the day, but the sky disagreed. The time for storms was now.

As they began the long climb up KY-207, Dee reached for the electrolyte bottle locked in her belt. The thermos wouldn't budge. The hill steepened. Eric surged ahead, attacking the incline exactly as she'd trained him: head down, arms pumping, feet quick and light.

"What the hell," Dee muttered, yanking harder at the stuck thermos. Thunder cracked. Rain dumped onto the road. Her grip tightened. Her focus narrowed. Control reasserted itself.

Eric shouldn't be pacing me.

She chased him, one arm twisted behind her back, pulling at the bottle as the asphalt slicked beneath her feet. She knew better than to be distracted on a hill in the rain. Her watch alarm screamed as her heart spiked. She didn't hear it over the thunder. She yanked again. The bottle came free.

The sudden release threw her forward. Her shoes slid. Her body pitched. Her shoulder hit first, dislocating instantly. Knuckles fractured. Her kneecap blew sideways. Her chin slammed down. Teeth crushed through tongue. Blood flooded her mouth. Pain tore through her. The road tilted away. She called out through her bloody throat.

"EWIC!"

But he didn't hear her. He'd already crested the hill.

At the bottom of the incline, a battered Ford Torino barreled through the rain. The driver fiddled with the radio, hungover and high, steering with his knees while checking for reception. Rain streaked the windshield. The wipers barely worked. Up ahead, Dee lay in a pile on the road.

Eric turned back at the crest. Dee should have been there. She always was.

"Dee?"

He ran downhill. Rain blinded him. Then he saw them. The car. The body. The intersection of both. He screamed and waved his arms. The driver looked up, panicked. He mistook Eric for a checkpoint cop, slammed the gas, yanked the wheel, and pulled a U-turn that fishtailed him across the road, missing Dee's head by inches before tearing off the other way.

Eric collapsed beside his wife.

"Dee!"

She breathed but didn't respond. Eric didn't bring his phone. Neither did Dee. Rain soaked their clothing. He begged his wife to wake up. When he tried to lift her, her body jerked. She screamed.

"NO!"

"I have to reset your shoulder," he said, voice steady despite the panic clawing at him.

"No— NO!"

He shoved the water bottle between her teeth then pushed her shoulder back into its socket. Dee's body jolted in agony. Her cry came out warped and trapped by plastic.

"I have to get you to a hospital." She was too numb to move. "One, two, three!"

Eric lifted her limp body with his knees. He was calm, practiced, as if this were a drill. He adjusted his grip and started down the road. Rain soaked them clean through. Blood smeared his shirt.

Dee tried to focus on something — the sound of his breathing, the rhythm of his steps — but sensation came in waves, crashing and receding before she could hold on to any one thing for long. Her arm dangled uselessly. Her leg throbbed. Her mouth filled with copper and spit. But Eric kept moving.

The road blurred. The sky darkened. Thunder rolled somewhere far off, then closer.

Dee squeezed her eyes shut and let go of trying to help, trying to direct, trying to endure. Her body did whatever it wanted. Pain and motion decided for her. She let herself be carried somewhere she didn't choose. She could no longer order it to stop.

34

___

Greenup General was once an office building. The city bought out an old engineering firm, repurposed the structure, and broke ground on Greenup's first and only hospital. It brought jobs, money, and healthcare to a town accustomed to doing without. The locals fondly called it Greenup G.

Greenup G was three stories. Babies occupied the top floor. Admitting and the ER filled the ground level. The second floor housed accidents, injuries, and surgeries that the locals called "Two." The basement held a morgue no one mentioned. That was where you went if you spent too much time on Two.

Dee lay in a hospital bed with her right arm in a sling, two fingers splinted, and five stitches binding her tongue. Steroids and painkillers kept her under, but gauze packed behind her lips forced her mouth closed — an unfamiliar restraint. Bandages dotted her face. Her left hand swelled, knuckles glazed in ointment. Her chest rose and fell in deep, steady sleep. The calm before the storm.

Eric sat in the room's only chair, an ancient wooden thing built to outlast comfort. Greenup G ran on state funding and stubbornness. Nothing matched. The X-ray machine looked prehistoric. Still, the doctors were competent and kind. That was all that mattered.

Doctor Seward entered with his hand out. "The husband?"

Eric lifted his palms, still stained with blood. "Yeah. Sorry."

Seward snapped his fingers and returned with sanitizing wipes. Eric scrubbed his hands, wiping his wife's blood from his skin.

"How is she?"

Seward flipped through the chart. "That tongue will hurt. The stitches will dissolve. She has a mild concussion." He paused. "Her shoulder may need surgery. Too early to say."

"What about her knee?"

"Patellar dislocation." Seward pulled back the sheet covering Dee. Her legs were swollen, bruised beyond hiding. One knee locked in a stabilizing brace, the other wrapped tight. "No weight for six weeks. After that, we'll reassess."

"She can't run?"

"She can't *walk*. Not right now, at least. Best-case scenario? Walking in six weeks. Running in a year."

"She'll miss the race."

Seward didn't respond. A nurse appeared at the door.

"Doctor Seward?"

He turned back to Eric. "Her fingers are fractured. Two to three weeks and they should heal. PT will follow. A nurse will go over her recovery." He held out his hand. Eric shook it.

When the room emptied, Eric stared at his wife. Depression pressed against his thoughts, heavy and inevitable. He thought about the story of Job. Loss layered on loss. All a test of faith. Eric took Dee's left hand in his, bowed his head, and knelt beside the bed and prayed.

I don't know why this keeps happening to her. I don't know how much more she can take. Please help her find peace. I can only do so much. I surrender this to you.

Eric squeezed her hand. She didn't stir. Her body lay immobilized, cataloged, and labeled. Schedules were added. Movement would be rationed now and prescribed in increments. But Dee loathed instructions.

Please help me win that race. Help us get through this. She needs hope. I need you. This will be bad.

The room hummed. Machines blinked. Somewhere in the hall, a cart rattled past. Dee remained unconscious while decisions about her body, her future, and her healing were decided for her again. Outside the window, the thunderstorm finally moved on. But inside the room, another storm was brewing.

35

———————

Dee woke from a twelve-hour pharmacologic sleep with a mouth like sandpaper and a hollow ache gnawing at her stomach. The room was dark. A thin strip of light leaked beneath the door. She smelled food before she saw it. Reaching, she hit something solid that groaned. Eric came into focus, folded into the wooden chair beside her bed, asleep. His head drooped toward an untouched meal tray balanced between them. Dee watched him for a moment, then looked away. She didn't want to wake him. She didn't want to see his face. Eric was a terrible liar. She'd know right away how badly she was injured. She closed her eyes and aimed her anger upward.

Right after my first orgasm. This is when You decide to step in?

Her stomach growled in response. The smell of warm cheese made her push her hand forward and try again. She reached past Eric, fingers brushing air, and shifted closer to the bed's edge. Pain flooded everywhere at once — knee, shoulder, back. She bore down, but her tongue was too swollen to seal her mouth. The tray crashed to the floor. Eric shot upright. Their eyes met. She knew immediately.

I can't run.

Dee shut her eyes.

Three times my life's collapsed this year. Four if you include marriage.

She rolled her head and pretended to sleep. Tears burned behind her eyes. Behind her eyelids, she spoke to God.

I hate You.

Eric hovered, uncertain if his wife was awake. When she didn't move again, he assumed sedation and sank into his chair, falling back to sleep.

Good, Dee thought. *I don't want to talk to him. And I definitely don't want to talk to Him.*

At home, Dee performed unconsciousness with discipline. She sat on the sofa, unmoving, eyes glazed, while Eric reorganized their lives around her injury. He placed protein powders and lotions within her now-hobbled reach.

A new pair of crutches sat beside the couch. Whenever Eric left the room, Dee stared at the metal underarms and imagined them snapping in half. When he returned, she resumed her vacancy. Playing dead felt easier than explaining herself. She'd started the act earlier, right after the orderly wheeled her down the halls of Two and said, "She'll be out of it for a while." Dee took notes on how to stay that way.

In the elevator, Eric accidentally pressed B instead of L.

"Whoops. Thought that B was for Bottom," he said as they landed in the basement morgue.

She wanted to scream at him. Instead, she cataloged another reason to hate life.

On the cab ride home, the driver took a sharp curve too fast. Dee's body slid despite the seatbelt. Pain detonated. Her mouth filled with curses. But she stayed silent.

The first time she *unconsciously* chose the act was during Dr. Seward's discharge instructions. She lay limp while Eric listened. Compression. Elevation. Weeks stacked up in Dee's head like prison bars. She squeaked, then let drool slide down her chin. No one questioned her. It was the medication, they thought. By the time they reached home, Dee spoke to no one for what felt like days. Once inside her house, anger drained out of her, leaving only exhaustion.

I may never speak again.

Eric watched her from the kitchen, hidden behind hanging baskets. He saw the way she glared at the crutches. The way she stiffened when he moved too close. He knew she was faking stupor.

Earlier, he'd provoked her, pressing B instead of L for Lobby, baiting her into correcting him. A feat she couldn't refuse. But Dee stayed dangerously mute. So Eric kept up her ruse, knowing better than to rush his wife.

Hours passed. Dee's body stayed still while her mind ran laps.

Three months without running will break me.

She told herself she would heal faster. That doctors always exaggerated. A jolt of agonizing heat surged in her leg.

Maybe not.

Missing the race wasn't the worst part.

He can't win without me. He'll skip workouts. He'll lose focus. He needs me.

Anger snapped inward. She spiraled. A colder voice answered.

This is because you indulged yourself instead of submitting to your husband, Lilith.

The name landed like a slap. She learned it as a teenager. Lilith Fair posters everywhere, women singing about bodies and freedom. Lilith was Adam's first wife. She was disobedient, then exiled and erased. A cautionary tale for women who refused submission — like Dee.

Repent!

Dee squeezed her eyes shut.

From the kitchen, Eric's phone rang. Words drifted toward her — *billing, insurance, denied.* The patio door slammed as he stepped outside. An ER visit alone could ruin them.

We're going to lose everything.

Her eyes opened. The voice sharpened.

Not unless you repent!

36

Eric stepped into the backyard so Dee wouldn't hear him arguing with the billing agent.

"I don't understand," he said, pacing the damp grass. "She was discharged yesterday."

Insurance confused him. Eric was used to universal healthcare. Long waits to see a doctor but no fees. In America, he carried an HMO. Emergency visits meant out-of-pocket robbery layered on top of referrals and runarounds. After Run Café became more hobby than business, Dee's $800 PPO premium was the first thing to go. The HMO was all they had. Now it was billing them dearly for it. Eric ended the call, wiped sweat from his forehead, and pulled his face into something resembling calm before going back inside.

"Want something to eat?" he asked, immediately realizing his mistake.

She won't answer.

He played it off, humming as he banged around the kitchen, opening and closing cabinets, making noise instead of thinking. Pots clanged. Busy sounded better than scared.

From the sofa, Dee listened.

If he were panicking, he wouldn't be humming, she thought. *He's not good at pretending. He's not a liar like me.*

Eric opened the same cabinet again.

What do you feed someone who can't talk or chew?

Guilt crept in.

It's my fault she fell.

The morning felt wrong from the start. The sky heavy, the air unsettled. Worry about the storm flickered but so had his excitement. Dee wanted sex. She wanted the run. He had given her both. As he laced his shoes that morning, something in him tightened. He didn't believe in intuition exactly, but he paused to ask if they should wait. He never shut Dee down. Especially not when things had finally been good. Their marriage was smoother. Sex was frequent. Dee was happier and more open than she'd ever been. He didn't want to be negative.

She would've ignored me anyway, he told himself. *Dee does what she wants.*

Eric dumped frozen bananas into the blender, his thoughts spinning with the blades.

What if we'd waited for the rain to pass? What if I'd said no?

The blender roared. He shut off the what-ifs.

I'm winning that race, he decided. *Our marriage depends on it.*

37

The first month of Dee's recovery tortured her. Without running, her body changed fast. Menopause and immobility tipped the scale. Dee weighed more than she ever did. The new number lodged in her brain like a personal failure. Her breasts grew heavy. Muscle drained away with shocking speed. Movement always kept her regulated. Without it, everything slid.

Her clothes betrayed her next. Bras cut into expanding flesh. Sports bras flattened and spilled her at the same time. Pants only buttoned if she lay down. Soon, she gave up entirely, moving on to sweatpants, then running shorts, and finally Eric's boxers and T-shirts. Roomy, anonymous, forgiving. Camouflage.

The more her body changed, the more she ate. The more she ate, the worse she felt. The cycle tightened daily.

At first, Dee watched Eric train. She told herself it was motivation. She'd heal. She'd come back stronger. She tracked his mileage mentally. Then envy set in. Eric left for long runs and returned slick with sweat, alive, rinsed clean by effort. She heard the shower run and clenched her jaw. She monitored his heart rate, watching it spike and settle on the Garmin she'd once controlled. With every mile he ran, Dee felt herself receding. Competition used to sharpen her. Now it hollowed her out.

She stopped paying attention. What replaced it was worse. She told herself Eric was stealing something that belonged to her first. That he only loved running to punish her. That his devotion was fake. That he was cheating. The stories felt real while she told them to herself.

She couldn't crutch to the car without gasping. Her knee throbbed. Her shoulder burned. Her body felt foreign, unreliable, and disobedient.

How does someone go from elite athlete to winded amateur walking to the bathroom?

The answer came easily.

Punishment.

As her resentment toward Eric grew, his fitness peaked. He ran more than ever, ate whatever he wanted, and stayed lean. His body sharpened while hers softened. She watched him with hatred.

Food changed too. Runner meals disappeared. Bananas and lentils gave way to fast food. McDonald's fit their budget. It numbed her faster. Eric's mileage absorbed it without consequence. Her body didn't. He became sculpted. She became something she refused to name. She avoided mirrors. She avoided people. Calls went unanswered. Flowers died on the porch. She screamed until their vases were shuttled back outside. She shut her phone off entirely.

Those people just want a story. Gossip.

The accusing voice fed her. Dee's only friend.

Leave him. This is his fault.

She was beginning to believe it.

Eric gave her space. He recognized the signs — injury, isolation, depression. He remembered being sidelined from hockey, the loneliness of watching teammates play without him. He avoided talking about his runs. He cooked, cleaned, and let Dee be.

Chapter 37

For better or worse. In sickness and in health.

He still wanted her. That had not changed. Her body — softer and heavier now — pulled his eyes the same as always. When she bent to grab a dropped crutch or reached for something on the counter, his gaze lingered. Dee noticed.

Good luck with that.

Sex was the last thing she wanted. She didn't want to see her own body naked. She didn't want to be touched. Didn't want to feel anything she couldn't immediately shut down. But she understood something else clearly: without sex, Eric's training would suffer. His focus would slip. His race would unravel. She held that knowledge gingerly. Whether the thought came from her mind or something darker, she didn't try to stop it.

It was the one thing she still could control.

38

Eric returned home from a hot thirty-miler in the September sun. His shirt and shorts clung to him, exposing taut, defined leg and back muscles honed from long mileage and steep hills.

Dee watched him peel off each layer, fuming with jealousy. A surge of violence shot through her. He was doused with sweat and salt she should've been bearing herself.

Make him pay, the voice inside her snarled.

"Come here," Dee barked.

Her cruelty made Eric quickstep from the bathroom to the side of the bed where his wife lay. Her oversized tee rippled around her large breasts and softening belly. One injured leg rested on a stack of pillows. Her bare foot hung off the mattress, toes wiggling, painted black with ancient, clumped polish she'd dug from the deepest cavern of her vanity drawer.

Pedicures always felt like a wasted luxury on endurance runners. But, immobile, Dee grew tired of staring at her ugly, coarse feet. She'd spent an entire afternoon cutting, filing, shaping, and painting. The poor-girl pedicure didn't last. Her feet looked as wrong as ever.

Eric stood shirtless at her bedside, wet from his run. Running had reshaped him completely, from brickhouse to Superman. Dee drank him in and recoiled from herself in the same breath. Everything he ate became fuel. Even garbage. Unlike her menopausal body — which converted even celery to fat — her husband had a romance-novel body.

And here I am turning into Jabba the Hutt.

Her eyes traced the sharp ridges of his Adonis belt.

He'll leave me eventually.

Dee's malice surged. She lifted her mangled foot toward his face and told him.

"Suck my toes."

Eric's jaw fell open. The thought made his tongue quiver. He'd done plenty in bed before — he had a girlfriend who was incredibly freaky — but this was different. Where it felt like that ex only wanted him for sex, Dee was nothing of the sort. Despite his sweat-soaked underwear, Eric grew hard at the thought of trying something new with his wife.

But toes?

The fetish both stimulated and repulsed him. Sucking on any part of Dee always stiffened him, but feet were dirty. Particularly Dee's. She'd been laid up for nearly two months. He'd noticed the dirt-caked soles. The bunions. The acrid odor he kept to himself.

Since her fall, Dee had cut off all intimacy like an electrician snapping a wire. Eric ached for her. Running dulled the need. Coming home exhausted helped too. Not that he'd have refused her if she wanted him. But she hadn't, and now she did, so he shut off his mind.

"Which toe?"

It was Dee's turn to be shocked. She'd expected disgust, refusal, a fight. Something she could use to push him away. Maybe forever. Not that she really wanted that.

He'll leave me anyway. This just speeds it up. When he goes, it'll be his fault. He didn't give me what I wanted. He should've submitted to me.

Scripture automatically surfaced.

Husbands, live with your wives showing honor to the woman as the weaker vessel.

Dee laughed silently.

I'm anything but weak. I dominate this relationship. Everything good in Eric's life — his visa, his body, living rent-free — is because of me. He owes me.

The dry space between her legs grew slick as the power rush swelled. Anticipating making her husband do something that repulsed him intoxicated her.

I'm no submissive wife. He does what I say.

And Eric always had. Dee directed him where to shop, how to load the dishwasher, when to water the garden. He never argued. He just listened, obedient. Like a good boy. Like a dog.

The power always rested in her fist. Now it rested in her foot.

She wiggled her left big toe. "This one."

Eric took her foot in his hands. The black polish flecked skin around the nail bed — sloppy, rushed, limited by her stiff shoulder and worsening eyesight. He'd noticed the typos in her texts lately, too. He said nothing about any of it.

Telling Dee what to do sparks fights. If something's wrong, she'll fix it herself.

The messy polish made him smile. Her imperfections delighted him. He'd always wondered what someone so beautiful and capable was doing with him. Any flaw of hers felt like mercy. It was only a matter of time before she realized he was a dud and left.

Eric bent and kissed her big toe. He tested the smell, the taste — no revulsion. Her skin was soft. Her lotion smelled like chocolate. He dove in. His tongue worked over all five toes, lapping at the webbing the way he once spread her thighs. Eric shifted to her smallest toe — chipped, painted with the most care.

Don't think. Just do what she tells you.

***

Dee stayed rigid. She squeezed her legs together, gathering wetness in her panties. Eric stayed bent over her, too absorbed to see her face contort. She resisted the urge to moan. She didn't want him to know she was about to come.

He must not give me pleasure, she repeated, mantra-like, willing her body to hold its bursting need.

Her back pressed into the headboard as Eric licked and sucked at her baby toe. Her angry façade collapsed. Jealousy had driven her. Punishment the goal. But the force overshot and arched straight into her erogenous zones. Dee clenched hard, fluid curling into the folds of her skin. She went rigid, holding herself at the edge. She wanted the orgasm but refused to give Eric the satisfaction.

This is foreplay, the calm voice inside whispered.

"Shut up," Dee spat at it, shoving her foot deeper into Eric's face.

39

A new obsession bloomed out of the dead bedroom of Dee's heart. She had her first orgasm the day she fell, but the brief release didn't compare to what followed: the ache of withholding, the compression of desire, the charge she felt feeding on Eric's docility. Pleasure delayed tasted much better than climax.

Whenever Eric left for work or long runs, Dee scoured the internet, relying on private browsing, as she tumbled from one sub-dom rabbit hole to the next. Curiosity slid easily into something from which she sensed she might not ever retreat.

In one forum, she learned communication sat at the center of sexual power — a skill she lacked, therefore had no interest in. On another, she read testimonies of abuse, misogyny, dysfunction, and danger. The sub-dom dynamic pulsed with opposites. Dee read on.

One testimony out of all of them stayed with her. An older woman. Married fifty years. Grown children. Separate bedrooms on separate floors. Love still lived between the spouses, but sex had vanished entirely decades ago. One day, angry over something small, the woman threw a shoe at her husband. When it hit his arm, he collapsed theatrically. She stood over him and spanked him with the shoe. Her pretend blows soon turned real.

Instead of taking offense, he loved it. He rolled onto his belly and invited her to keep going. A dust-up edged with dominance and submission. Their faux fight jolted their sex life awake. Now, their intimacy was built around spanking — something they never would have discovered without that thrown shoe.

This is not me, Dee thought.

She scrolled for something more relatable. After a few graphic testimonies, she snapped her laptop shut, hoping to scrub the entire fetish from her mind. Still, the shoe story lingered. Mostly because Dee had stumbled into sexual dominance accidentally, too. The idea refused to settle inside her. It was abnormal. As powerful as her stifled orgasm felt, taking pleasure from it felt secretive, dishonest, and unfaithful.

But to who?

She chalked up her curiosity to being too taboo. The entire world of kink felt like WPC — White People Crap — as her dad Morris sometimes called it. He muttered the term after long days dealing with impossible clients. A homeowner demanding rare marble sourced from a specific Italian mountain, quarried only when the moon and the stars aligned, wasn't discerning. They were wasting Morris's time. Time equaled money. Everyone understood that except White people who believed they controlled both. WPC was unnecessary, ostentatious, and vulgar. And that was exactly how the sub-dom culture made Dee feel.

Would Daddy think me marrying a White man was WPC too?

Race was always openly discussed in the Moreland house. Mavis and Morris expected — if not demanded — that their daughters marry Black men. Sometimes it felt like the rest of the world agreed.

I've felt judged just standing beside Eric.

Race. Sex. Money. Dee measured her marriage against the countless online accounts of sexless couples who stumbled into kink and rediscovered desire.

Maybe this could give us a chance.

The thought barely formed before discomfort dragged her back.

Anything that requires someone to be called a slave *is everything I am not. My ancestors would roll in their graves.*

Guilt piled onto her already aching body. Beneath the laptop, Dee squeezed her legs together, as if she could pull the wetness back inside herself. Still, the seed was planted. Scripture rose up like a weed.

The body is not meant for sexual immorality...

The Bible demanded she honor her body.

But isn't enjoying my husband a gift too?

Unholy, improper, and knee-deep in White People Crap, Dee wanted to tear the Good Book apart with her teeth.

How can something feel so good and so bad at the same time?

Religion pressed down on her.

Repent.

Aging hurt her body and fantasy twisted her mind. Together, they diminished her until surrender felt like the only option. She tried to drop into a double genuflection, but her knee stopped her short. She adjusted awkwardly, folding into an L-shape on the floor.

This is the best I can do.

She rushed through her prayer. Adoration felt impossible.

You know everything. You see everything.

Confession came fast. Her mind replayed the morning, watching Eric dress, imagining stilettos, kicks to his ribs, an orgasm based on domination, then stopping short to later dirty her mind online. But not all of it was filth. Scrolling a discussion board, Dee learned she had an innie vulva. Page after page cracked open questions she'd never been allowed to ask. On these sites, knowledge equaled power. She was learning how her own body worked. She wanted to understand and not understand at the same time. But she wouldn't let herself orgasm, though she was naturally supposed to. Shame arrived well before pleasure could ever make it in the door. She invoked Onan, who spilled his own seed, then was killed for being wicked.

I've lost my family, my running, my business, but not my life. Is that next?

From confession she rushed into thanksgiving.

Thank You for my home, my car, the internet.

Then supplication.

Please don't send me to Hell.

She asked for nothing else. No healing, no relief. Dee Taylor only begged to not be exiled like Lilith. Not to be struck down like Onan. Not to be cast out as a pervert for nearly orgasming after making her husband suck a toe. She prayed Numbers 6:24–26. Peace in exchange for denial. The trade felt wildly unbalanced. Still, no lightning bolt arrived.

Confused, Dee hobbled to the couch. She shut down incognito mode, closing twenty-three tabs. Then she opened a fresh window — one that would appear plainly in her history should anyone look — and typed: CHURCH NEAR ME.

40

Dee's new interest in sex wasn't White People Crap, it was Dee's crap, and it wasn't crap at all. Scripture condemned her curiosity, but she needed release. With Eric gone most days between work, hockey, and training for the now-weeks-away ultra, Dee built her life around his absence. She linked their Find My apps so she could track his whereabouts. She didn't question the relief she felt when his dot moved farther away from hers.

She went back online to fulfill her urge. The memory of Toe Day still worked. Reading other women's stories still worked. But when the pulse between her legs demanded attention, she limped to the bedroom and slid her healed hand between her thighs and found nothing. Her body stayed dry and distant. She stopped rubbing, irritated and embarrassed, and went back to the sofa to figure out why Eric and a toe could wake her body, but she couldn't do it herself. Dee didn't know how to touch herself and she was in her mid-forties. She felt stupid and late.

Instead, she moved forward with what she did know — discipline and control.

Each morning, she pretended to sleep while Eric dressed, cooked, brewed coffee, and left. After his van pulled away, she ate measured food, then claimed the sofa — her command center.

Chapter 40

From there she could erase evidence in seconds. She rubbed testosterone gel behind her thigh and searched for stories of women like her. Older, dry, and alive again. She hated how much she'd missed.

Why didn't I learn this sooner?

Desire returned while she read an article about having multiple sexual partners at once.

"That's called an orgy," she said aloud, impressing no one.

She thought about Eric's past lovers — how many, she didn't know.

"That's called a body count." She impressed no one again.

She knew she was the first Black woman Eric had ever been with, but the thought of him with any other woman made her stomach turn.

He's not only going to leave, but for someone who's nothing like you.

Anger, rage, jealousy, and shame closed the article. Dee opened Google and typed: PORN.

Scripture grabbed hold of her.

God will not let you be tempted beyond what you can bear.

"Screw that," Dee said, hitting return.

The first site loaded a grid of White bodies mid-act. Endless White bodies. She scrolled fast, unsettled. By page thirteen, she found a Black woman not labeled "ebony" or "exotic." Their performance repelled her. Too loud. Too wet. Too much. She closed the site.

The second site was worse. No Black women at all. She pressed X out of the page and tried again.

The third site was animated. Monsters, demons, absurd bodies with unreal proportions. Her shoulders dropped with relief. This felt safer. She clicked on a video — an animated creature towering over a woman. Dominance exaggerated. Consent unmistakable. Despite being a cartoon, something deep inside Dee stirred.

"This is what turns me on?"

She carried the laptop to the bed before the feeling disappeared. Shorts stayed on. Ankles crossed. Hands pressed together between her thighs.

This is wrong.

Her thoughts moved fast. Monster. Maiden. Power. Yield.

Yes, it's wrong. It bad. It's—

Dee bucked hard against the mattress and came, sudden and violent, breath knocked clean out of her. She froze.

I did it. I masturbated myself to orgasm.

The pride lasted seconds. Shame rushed in quick, hot, and merciless. She lay still, staring at the ceiling, eyes filling with tears.

What have you done, you shameful girl?

Day after day, Eric remained oblivious while Dee ransacked the internet for monster porn. He filled his time with work, running, shopping, cleaning, cooking, and paying bills, while she filled hers with masturbation and repentance-watching sermons on sin. Their marriage settled into a rhythm of don't ask, don't tell.

One Saturday, Eric made Dee an egg-white omelet and watched her laugh at something on her phone.

She scrolled, trying to cool the heat between her thighs.

I hope he leaves. I want a quickie with myself.

The thought relaxed her with its ease.

Months ago, this would've horrified me. Now it feels necessary.

Sometimes guilt flickered. She always pushed it aside and kept scrolling.

I'm allowed to want this. This is healthy.

Her tools helped. Her body responded. The problem was simple: Eric didn't know. She pushed the dilators further. Overdid the testosterone. Dark, coarse hair sprouted where the gel pooled on her hamstring.

Eric's penis still worked. He would've liked to be part of her exploration. Or at least to know about it. By keeping him out, Dee tightened something brittle. As Eric cooked, Dee waited for him to leave. After promising herself she'd quit animated porn, curiosity dragged her back the very next day. Her laptop reopened and monsters returned. Days turned to weeks.

It's wrong. It's filthy. Marriage should be honored...

Dee responded to her thoughts. *I'm not hurting anyone. I'm not cheating. I just need this.*

To soothe herself, Dee streamed sermons from an all-Black church.

Am I acting justly? Am I loving my husband?

She knew the answer. Her body pulsed on schedule now. Weekdays meant Incognito Mode. Weekends meant waiting, pretending to nap. The lie became routine. Alone, she felt alive. When Eric came home, her energy dropped. His presence turned her privacy into a cage.

Eric flipped eggs, scratching at the rash blooming on his wrist.

"It's just eczema," he said.

I just want her to touch me, he thought. *I just want to feel wanted.*

He watched Dee giggle at her phone.

She's been happier lately. Even if it's not with me.

That Saturday, Dee's impatience spiked.

"Can you go to the store?" she asked.

"Now?"

"I need aspirin." She pressed her injury like leverage.

He brought her a bottle. She tried again.

"Aren't you running today?"

"If you want me gone, just say so."

"I don't care if you're here," Dee snapped, anger flaring too fast.

The day iced over. By nightfall, guilt returned — duty, submission, and obligation.

Only I can fix him. Only I can relieve him. Our entire relationship is on me.

She avoided the bedroom and chose to sleep on the sofa. Eric spooned pillows. His teeth ground. His skin flared. She ignored all the signs.

You're a horrible wife.

Invisibility felt safer than intimacy. She tiptoed into the bedroom after he fell asleep and changed in the closet, hiding her body.

I wish I'd never gotten married.

Eric stayed still, pretending to sleep.

I love her, he thought. *She's just going through it.*

Dee went back to the sofa, slid her hand beneath her waistband, and closed her eyes.

Eric can't pleasure me like I can.

In the bedroom, her husband lay awake.

42

———

Dee woke to the slam of cabinet doors. Darkness pressed against the windows. The wall clock read 6:40. Eric's heavy footsteps crossed the hardwood, louder than usual. Dee hauled herself off the sofa and limped toward the noise.

"Eric?" she called. Her voice came out thin.

He stood at the stove in night-running gear, reflective vest strapped tight across his torso. Dee recognized it immediately. It was hers. Her gaze dropped to the counter. Her Garmin sat there, screen glowing, angled toward him.

"Have you been tracking me?" Eric asked. No greeting, no concern. Just the question.

"Sure. We track each other on our phones."

"That's not what I mean." His voice was sharp.

Dee knew exactly what he meant, but she didn't understand why he was this upset.

Yeah, I tracked his vitals. That's normal. That's supportive.

She lifted her chin. "Of course I tracked you. I needed to make sure you weren't going to have a heart attack."

Eric picked up the watch and held it between them. "You weren't tracking my vitals. You were manipulating them. How?"

Chapter 42

Dee's stomach flipped. *Does he know?* She shoved the fear down and away.

"Manipulating is dramatic. I'm coaching you. Tracking your progress."

Eric laughed without humor. He tossed a banana into the blender, followed by protein powder and soy milk. His movements were angry; his face wasn't. That worried her more.

"If you didn't think I was capable of running, why'd you let me start in the first place?"

Dee slid onto a stool and softened her expression as she clocked his mood. Irritability, hunger, projection. She pulled on her nurturing mask like armor. "Something happen out there?"

"All this running," Eric snapped, slamming the cabinet shut. "I hate it."

"Bad runs happen. They're part of growth."

"That doesn't explain why you're controlling my heart rate."

He was right, but Dee wasn't about to admit it.

Eric paced the floor. His watch died fifteen miles in. When he came home, he found Dee's did too. She synced their trackers.

Not just tracking me. Directing *me.*

He stopped pacing and faced her. "Do you have any idea what it feels like to realize your wife is adjusting your body from afar?"

Dee waited for her turn to speak. This wasn't it. She let him continue.

"We don't talk. We don't touch. You don't kiss me hello or goodbye anymore. Not because I stopped trying. Because you did." His voice cracked. "All you care about is this damn race." The blender roared to life, filling the space between them with noise.

Dee weighed the truth. Masturbation. Porn. Marriage. Divorce. The cost was catastrophic. The reality worse.

If I tell him everything, something breaks forever. If I say nothing, something already has.

Every scenario twisted her stomach into knots. She froze, unable to step out of the boat and trust she could walk on water.

Eric stood, ready to offer forgiveness before she'd even asked for it. He gave her time, space, and grace. He'd done everything right. He was the dream husband. Or so he thought.

So why do I feel so trapped?

Dee opened her mouth.

This could help us. This could change everything.

But nothing came out.

Eric's hand hovered over the Vitamix switch, tense and waiting.

Finally, Dee exhaled. "I'm sorry for monitoring your progress. I would never want to do anything to intentionally harm you." The words surprised her. Soft, affectionate, and uncharacteristic. She wanted to take them back. They weren't true.

Eric's shoulders slumped. Relief softened his jaw. He turned off the blender. "I want to be mad, but your apology helps." He met her eyes. "I forgive you. I'm sorry too."

He reached across the narrow island and took her hand.

Something tight and thorny twisted in Dee. Climbing her throat, choking off any reply.

He has nothing to apologize for. He's being vulnerable. Why can't I?

The feeling dissolved, leaving words locked inside her. She held his hand.

Help me, she thought.

The kitchen hummed. Outside darkness crept through the blinds. Dee sat, Eric's warm hand in hers, while something essential sank quietly out of reach.

Oh, ye of little faith. Why did you doubt?

43

―――――

Eric let himself be tracked, acting as if nothing happened. No confrontation. No suspicion. No acknowledgment that his wife hadn't slept with him in nearly three months. By early October, Dee gained another ten pounds. Acne spread across her back and butt. Eric avoided any mention of weight, running, or skin. He had learned those were live wires and stepped cautiously.

Dee stopped doubting like Peter and started enduring like Job. But really, she didn't care which biblical figure applied anymore. She didn't care about the Bible at all.

I prefer the forbidden.

She stopped watching sermons. She stopped trying to be good. When guilt surfaced, she crushed it with spite.

Why didn't You just kill me with my family? Why let me live? This is all Your fault.

When Eric came home, Dee wanted to scream, nag, or disappear. Sometimes he sat in the car before coming inside, whispering to himself: *This will pass.* Other times, he cried with his forehead against the steering wheel. He didn't want to go inside Dee's house as much as she didn't want him there.

At least we have one thing in common.

One Sunday, home alone, Dee typed "punishment" into a

porn site's search bar. The results were brutal. Pleasure stripped of anything tender. She hovered over thumbnails, assessing. No arousal yet, just appetite.

Eric left for a long run. Dee tracked him until she was sure he was far enough away. The house felt empty even when they were both in it. They barely spoke anymore.

Dee tried to watch. Tried to finish. Her body wouldn't cooperate. Everything felt fake. The moans. The movements. The repetition.

Why does none of this feel real?

She closed the laptop and slid it under her pillow.

I'm done.

She meant it this time. No more porn. No more animated sex. No more masturbation. It wasn't doing anything for her anyway. That first time was what she was always chasing. Everything was downhill since the first time she'd made herself come.

Dee stared out the bedroom window. The glass was spotless. Eric cleaned it. He cleaned everything. Even raked the yard. Details she never acknowledged. The property was immaculate. Like a life someone else was tending. She didn't thank him. She didn't even notice until now.

Her mind drifted to Run Café. The races pinned to the wall. Running through heat and cold. The way movement once made her feel alive. She lay back on the bed. Pimply, heavy, and lonely. She felt like the physical proof of disobedience.

Outside, the Sandy River slid past the house. Colorful leaves sat bright on the trees. The land looked vibrant and cared for. Something in her loosened.

Maybe my life isn't over. Maybe I just stopped showing up.

She spoke aloud:. "Poor Eric. I should thank him."

A surge of desire followed. Faint but present. She wanted one last time alone. She removed her laptop from under her pillow and clicked the first video on her favorite site. It wasn't even a sex theme she liked. She just wanted it over with. One last time before going cold turkey. She positioned herself. Hands between her legs. Head on a pillow.

This will be quick. Then I'll shower. Then I'll start fixing things.

She didn't hear the front door open. The sounds from the screen filled the room. Her body finally responded. Her mouth opened, matching the noise she'd been listening to.

"What the fuck are you doing?"

Eric stood in the doorway. It was the first time Dee ever heard him use the F-word. It wouldn't be the last.

Eric heard it before he saw it. Not music, not television. It was rhythmic. Intimate. It cut through him before his mind could refuse it.

Someone's having sex.

He stopped in the doorway. Dee on the bed. Laptop open. Light from the screen flickering across her face. Her hands between her legs. Mouth open, matching the noise she'd been listening to.

She's cheating.

His heart fluttered. The room sharpened into fragments: his sweatpants she wore, his pillow under her head, the glow of the screen. The sound was obscene in its persistence.

"What the fuck are you doing?!"

The words came out angry, stripped of restraint.

"Eric!"

Dee jolted upright, scrambling. She slammed the laptop shut like it could erase what he'd seen. Her voice rushed ahead of her thoughts.

"It's not what you think."

"The fuck it's not!" The cursing came easy now. It sounded

like someone else's voice. His heart hammered. Rage filled him. He stepped into the room, finally moving.

"Porn, Dee? Really?"

Her face hardened, defensive and cornered. "You don't understand."

The words landed worse, somehow. He knew this excuse. He invented it.

"Oh, I understand."

"You're acting like I betrayed you."

"Fuck you!"

It was low and brutal. He'd heard the same phrase hurled at him plenty of times, but he'd never once said it to her. He saw it land. The way her shoulders jerked. The way her face closed. "You don't get to tell me how I feel!"

"Okay, but I know how you feel about betrayal," Dee said. "This isn't cheating."

He shook his head. His body hurt. Adrenaline drained out of him, leaving him hollow and scared. He looked at the bed, the laptop, the place where he was supposed to feel safe. He wanted to leave. He wanted to scream. He wanted to collapse on the floor and drown in the carpet. Instead, he waited for the world to split open and make the next move. The moans from the video were the only sounds he heard.

45

Neither slept. Doors slammed. Tears came in waves. Mostly Eric's.

"You cheated!"

"It was just me, Eric. There wasn't anyone else."

Eric paced, hands pressed to his temples. "Why didn't you just come to me? Or at least talk to me?"

Dee snapped. "I want my life back! I want control over what happens to me."

He stopped pacing. "Godly people don't do this."

That did it.

"Where was God when my family died? Where was He when my body broke? I don't even know if I ever believed in a God."

Eric stared at her like she'd suddenly morphed into someone else.

They circled until vitriolic words ran out. Eric left the room. Dee grabbed her keys.

"Where are you going?" he asked, trying not to beg. She didn't answer.

Outside, the night was moonless. Dee drove with no destination, just distance. Her shoulder throbbed as she turned the wheel. Pain didn't stop her anymore. She followed the road without deciding to. The Mini Mall Marketplace appeared out of

144

the dark. Dee pulled into her old spot and killed the engine. Run Café sat shuttered, a "for lease" sign in the window, dust on the glass. So much silence where life used to hum — albeit quietly.

She stepped out of the car. Crickets filled the air. The building looked smaller than she remembered. Tired, she stood on the steps and stared through the window. The bell still hung inside. The place looked neglected, just like it had always been.

I let this happen.

Her stomach lurched. Dee leaned over the railing and vomited, hard and fast, emptying more than her gut. When it passed, she sank onto the steps.

"I did this," she said.

The café. The marriage. The slow retreat from responsibility. She saw it clearly now.

"I'm the problem."

The crickets stilled. Dee pressed her palms together and bowed her head.

"I know I don't deserve mercy, but I need it."

She spoke with no bargaining, no vows, just need. From behind her, headlights flared. Dee didn't turn around. She already knew who it was.

Eric sat on the sofa long after Dee left. The house felt wrong without her noise, even when that noise was anger.

Her on the bed. The screen. The sound. Humiliation burned hotter than rage. He stood, paced, stopped, and prayed. He wanted to be righteous. He wanted to forgive Dee immediately just so the hurt would stop. He thought about what she'd said: about God, about control, about wanting her life back. He didn't recognize his marriage anymore.

He'd driven to the café countless times. Dee next to him talking about runners and dreams. This time he drove alone. He pulled into the lot and saw her car. Relief and dread hit at the same time.

Dee sat on the steps, shoulders slumped. She looked smaller than he remembered. Eric cut the engine and stepped out.

"Dee."

She flinched but didn't look up. He walked closer. He didn't reach for her.

"I didn't come to fix anything. I just needed to know where you were." The building hovered behind them like a silent third body. "I can't pretend that this didn't happen."

"I'm not asking you to."

Chapter 46

Eric looked at the café. The dust, the sign, the loss. "I still love you, but I'm hurt and I'm angry. I don't know who you are right now."

"I'm trying to figure that out too."

He exhaled. "We can't keep lying to each other."

Dee finally looked up at him. Her eyes were wrecked. "I know."

His lips spread into a smile. Not with forgiveness or rejection. Just acceptance.

"Come home," he said. "We'll decide what happens next when it's light."

After a moment, Dee stood. They walked back to their cars side by side. For the first time in years, Dee didn't try to be holy. She didn't lie. She didn't deflect. She tried to be real.

47

———

Dee clasped her hands in her lap, fingers locked tight. Her white silicone wedding ring shimmered under the track lighting of Dr. Jan Ryerson's office. Twenty-five dollars a session for marriage counseling, thanks to Eric's HMO.

They sat on opposite ends of the couch. Dee was already defensive. She could feel it in her jaw. Her face already decided it was the place to brace.

Dr. Ryerson glanced between them. "Eric, can you tell me what brought you here?"

"I walked in on my wife masturbating to porn after months of not touching me."

Dee flinched. Her first instinct was to justify her action. To explain the context. The loneliness. The menopause and pain. She stuffed it all down.

"It wasn't the porn that made me so mad," Eric continued. "It was the secrecy. I felt humiliated and replaced." His eyes closed with the memory. "It triggered all my worst fears from my childhood."

"And what are those fears?"

Eric blinked. "That she wanted something I couldn't give her and had to find it somewhere else."

Chapter 47

The sentence hung between them. Dee stared at the carpet, suddenly finding it incredibly fascinating. Her pulse thudded in her ears. Ryerson turned to her.

"Dee, what do you think about what Eric just shared?"

"I'm ashamed," Dee said. The word felt blunt. She paused, feeling the urge to soften it. To sound kinder than she was. She didn't. "I didn't think about how it would hurt him."

Eric looked at her, startled.

"So, you weren't trying to hurt him," Ryerson said. "But you did."

"Yes."

Eric nodded his agreement.

Ryerson inhaled. "I want to try something. It's called a soft startup." Dee nearly laughed. The phrase sounded so clinical and basic. She thought of her pelvic wand. "Dee, I want you to express a need without criticism, blame, or explanation. Just a need of yours."

Dee's throat tightened. It was like when Eric asked what she wanted when they were intimate. She never had a clean answer. What she needed felt messy. A need reduced to a sentence felt like a lie.

"I need..." She stopped, reconsidered, tried again. "I need him to stop acting like I'm some problem to solve."

Eric's shoulders stiffened. He pressed his lips closed.

Ryerson raised a hand. "That's a criticism. Try again."

Heat crawled up Dee's neck. "I need to feel safe. Even when I'm not."

Eric stared at the floor this time.

"Eric," Ryerson said, "reflect back what you heard. Not what you think she meant. Just what she said."

"You need to feel safe, even when you're not."

"How was that?" Ryerson asked.

"Awful," Dee said.

Ryerson gave a small nod. "Honesty can feel uncomfortable."

Dee had urges to explain herself. Eric saw red. A new emotion for him. They sat, neither of them reaching for resolution.

"What do you want now?" Ryerson asked.

Eric answered first. "I want to stop pretending this didn't matter."

"It does matter," Dee shot back.

Dr. Ryerson folded her hands. "Then this is where we start."

48

Dr. Ryerson opened her notebook. "Before we begin, I want to talk about intimacy homework."

Dee felt it in her body before her mind. The familiar clamp in her pelvis at the thought of sex with her husband. Beside her, Eric shifted uncomfortably too.

"I'd like you to practice non-goal-oriented intimacy," Ryerson continued, using the same hot-button word. "Touch without expectation. No pressure for intercourse."

Dee let out a humorless laugh.

Eric turned toward her. "What?"

"Pressure," Dee said. "It's all pressure. I can't *practice* intimacy like it's yoga. My body doesn't work that way."

Ryerson looked at her. "Tell us more about that."

Dee's hands curled into fists. "I can't order myself to be turned on. Penetration hurts." Ryerson's eyebrows lifted. She gave Dee a look.

Go on.

"It feels like I'm being split open. It's like bone on bone. There's no pleasure there."

"Then how were you doing it before your accident?" Eric countered.

151

"Because I—"

"Let's slow this down. One issue at a time," Ryerson saved her. "Eric, I want you to reflect what Dee just said."

"I don't want to reflect," he snapped. "I want to understand why my wife won't have sex with me when she used to just fine."

"Wow. There it is," Dee's voice shook. "Won't. Like I'm refusing you."

"That's not what I said."

"It's what you mean."

"Dee," Ryerson interrupted. "What does this bring up for you without assigning intent?"

Dee snorted. "Want me to say it nicely?"

"I want you to say it *clearly*."

"Fine." She inhaled. "I was taught that my body belongs to my husband. That if I say no, I'm failing as a wife."

Eric's jaw slackened. "Who taught you that?"

Dee's voice rose. "Submit yourselves unto your own husbands. Ephesians 5:22."

Ryerson shifted in her seat. "Now, I'm not equipped to talk—"

"That's the whole problem," Dee cut in. "This isn't about communication. It's scripture. Obedience! It's telling me to just lie there and let my husband have his way with me because that's what a good wife does."

Eric stood up. "That's not what I want!"

"Then why do you keep asking and forcing me?"

"That's not true!"

"Both of you, stop!"

They didn't. Eric turned fully toward Dee. "You don't touch me. Then I walk in and you're watching some sick fucking porno—"

"You hurt," Dee shouted back. "You hurt me! Every time you push, every time you sigh, every time you act like I still owe you access to my body hurts!"

"Jesus! You're making it sound like I raped you!"

Chapter 48

"Because sometimes it feels like you are!"

Eric looked like he'd been slapped. Ryerson stood.

"I'm going to press pause."

Eric grabbed Dee's arm, stopping her from walking out.

"This level of conflict is beyond the scope of traditional couples' therapy," Ryerson said. "It's beyond the scope of my training. We need to bring in another professional. Someone trained specifically in sexual health and desire. This isn't about who's right. It's about safety."

Dee stared at the floor.

Safety.

The word felt theoretical. It felt like WPC.

In the parking lot, Eric paced. Dee sat in her car and pressed her forehead to the steering wheel. She felt exactly as she did before therapy — smaller and trapped.

Submit.

The word rang in her head, heavy and cruel.

49

***

South Point, Ohio sat thirty minutes from Greenup. Dee liked that. No chance of running into someone she knew while unpacking the most private parts of herself.

Rebekah Carr's office was warm and sparse. No posters, no inspirational quotes. Just a low couch, two chairs, and a box of tissues.

"What brings you in?" Rebekah asked.

Dee glanced at Eric, then at the floor. "Porn," she said. "Intimacy."

"Tell me what porn does for you." Rebekah directed the question at Eric.

"Not me. Her."

Eric pointed at Dee. Her eyes pulled to a squint.

"Please forgive my assumption," Rebekah said uncomfortably. "Dee, what does porn do for you?"

"Control," Dee said, half-cutting Rebekah off. "I don't have to be naked. I don't have to perform. I don't have to be rejected or pressured. I can do and feel what I want."

Eric's jaws clenched.

"So porn is about safety," Rebekah said. Dee's hands balled up into fists. "When did intimacy stop feeling safe?"

Chapter 49

"It never was," Dee bit back. "I grew up believing sex was dangerous and sinful. That desire led to destruction. Like Lilith."

Eric turned toward her. He'd never heard this before. Rebekah lifted her chin. She had.

"I learned how to say no before I ever learned how to want," Dee continued. "By the time I was married, sex felt like an obligation. Pleasure and desire weren't mine. Just compliance."

"That's common in a purity-culture upbringing," Rebekah said. Dee stiffened. "You said you were raised religious?" Dee blushed and nodded. Eric watched her every move. "When you watch porn, what are you looking for?"

"Power," Dee said, straight at her husband. "Dominance. Sometimes nothing specific. I'm trying to figure it out."

"And how do you feel afterward?"

"Relieved," Dee said. "Then ashamed."

"That tells me porn is doing two jobs," Rebekah said. "One helpful, one harmful."

"Helpful?" Dee sat straighter. "So porn isn't bad?"

"It's a tool," Rebekah said. "But secrecy turns it corrosive. And addiction shuts the other partner out."

Eric's body language agreed with her.

"In your case, porn became a substitute instead of a supplement. That's what mimics betrayal."

"How is discovering myself a betrayal?" Dee asked. "It makes me feel behind."

"You're not behind. You're delayed."

Delayed. The word landed like it was judging her.

"I don't want you saying yes to sex if you don't want it," Rebekah said. "I also don't want you disappearing into porn. What I want is curiosity."

"About what?" Dee asked.

"About your desire," Rebekah said. "Not Eric's. Yours."

Dee felt her body recoil at the ownership. Next to her, Eric recrossed his legs.

"Curiosity sounds indulgent," Dee said. "Like something

only White women get." Rebekah didn't interrupt. "Curiosity is how I got in trouble. It doesn't feel natural. I don't have the luxury of being curious. I'm too *delayed.*"

"That makes sense," Rebekah said. "Given what curiosity has cost you." Her eyes landed on Eric. He lowered his head.

"I'm not asking you to act on desire," Rebekah continued. "I'm asking you to notice when it arises, how, and without fixing it. And then share this with Eric."

Dee felt naked and exposed. "That sounds hard and embarrassing."Eric looked at her tentatively. "I'm scared if I tell him what I want, he'll judge me."

"I'm scared she doesn't want me at all," Eric said.

"Those fears mirror each other," Rebekah said. "For now, just notice your desire."

When Dee and Eric left, nothing was resolved. They didn't touch. But they also didn't fight. They simply didn't talk at all.

50

─────────

Eric kept both hands on the wheel. Dee watched the Kentucky roads slip by — the same stretches she'd run a hundred times. Oak, maple, sycamore. Familiar blurs, fast distractions.

At home, they moved around each other like planets in orbit. Close enough to feel the pull; far enough not to touch. Dinner was reheated leftovers. Eric ate at the kitchen counter. Dee in the living room, one foot propped on a pillow. She stayed on the couch, adjusting her position.

"Do you want to try the homework?" Eric called out.

Fear rose first. Dee shook her head, though he couldn't see her. "Okay."

He joined her on the sofa. They sat side by side, leaving a careful inch between them. Touch without expectation. After a moment, she reached for Eric's hand. The contact felt deliberate, awkward. Definitely not intimate. Eric let out a short breath through his nose and shifted his weight. She ignored it.

What she noticed first wasn't desire; it was tension. The steady urge to retreat inward. To disappear and leave. Eric squeezed her hand a little tighter.

Dee tried again. She closed her eyes and let an image surface — the kind she usually kept private. Her mind drifted briefly to her computer. Something stirred inside her. It didn't feel so much like a crime.

"I feel something," Dee said. "A want."

Eric's free hand rested on her upper thigh. She let it stay.

"Do you want me?" he asked.

The question killed the momentum. Dee opened her eyes.

"I don't like when you ask me that. If I want you. What I want. I don't have those words yet. Can't I just be?"

"I'm not trying to push," he said defensively. "I just—" He stopped. "I'm sorry."

The apology was sincere enough. Her body shut down anyway, leaving only the ache.

"When you ask me things like that, it feels like there's a right answer."

Eric let go of her hand. "I just need to know where I stand."

"That's the problem," Dee said. "I can't give you that with my words, or my body."

They sat saying nothing. After a moment, Eric spoke first.

"Maybe this was too soon."

Relief spread through Dee, loosening her breath. "Yeah. Too soon." She stood. "I'm going to shower."

In the bathroom, she locked the door and turned the water hot. Steam filled the room, softening the edges. Under the spray, her shoulders dropped. The ache returned, dull yet manageable. She resisted touching herself by turning the hot water cold.

Later, in bed, they lay on opposite sides. Dee stared at the ceiling, aware of her body in a way that didn't demand anything from her. After a while, she reached toward Eric and wrapped her arms around him — not to reassure him or fix anything. Just to rest as two spoons.

He exhaled and pulled her close without moving or asking for more. Relief came for them both. Not because anything worked, but because nothing was being asked of either.

51

———————

The church sat a few towns over and tucked behind a row of maples. Dee noticed the building before the sign. No steeple, no marquee announcing damnation or a Sunday-morning joke. Just a low brick structure with wide windows and a gravel lot.

"This is it," Eric said, pulling in.

Dee stayed still in her seat. She had not seen the inside of a church in a long time.

Inside, the room felt open. Light poured through stained glass windows. The congregation was mixed: Black families, White couples, and more. None of them stared. Dee slid into a pew near the back.

Pastor Marlena stepped to the front without ceremony. She read from Psalm 139.

Search me, God, and know my heart.

"This isn't a threat or something scary," Marlena said softly. "It's an invitation. To be known without being corrected for who you are. We spend so much time trying to be good, but goodness without honesty is just fear."

Dee pressed her lips together. Eric took her hand.

Marlena continued. "For some of us, faith was introduced

through control. Through silence. Through shame. That's not holiness. That's survival."

Dee's breath hitched. Eric noticed. This sermon was meant for her. After the service, Eric took Dee by her elbow.

"Want to say hello?"

Normally, Dee would've said no. Instead, she let herself be led. Marlena greeted her like a person, not a project. She shook Dee's hand and held it a second longer than expected.

"We have coffee. You look tired," Marlena said gently.

Dee laughed once. "I am."

They sat in the rectory without donuts or people.

"I don't know what I believe anymore," Dee said finally.

Marlena grinned. "That's normal."

"Is it?" Dee asked.

"It is. Most everyone struggles."

"Except Noah."

Marlena laughed. "That's true."

Dee hesitated. "I was taught questioning my faith was dangerous."

Marlena met her eyes. "Questioning isn't the problem. Silence is. That's when all the bad things happen."

Dee let that sit. "I'm angry at God."

"I would be too," Marlena said. "Loss changes the questions. Especially when it's our entire family that gets taken away from us."

Dee broke down. Marlena gave her a Kleenex and Dee took it.

"God isn't your enemy. I know it doesn't seem that way, but try to remember He's on your side."

At home that night, Dee sat on the edge of the bed mulling over her morning. The gentle sound of the shower cut through the silence. Her laptop sat next to her.

Is it really so bad if I just look?

She pushed the desire away, then closed her eyes and spoke to God.

52

Dee was on the living-room floor, counting small movements based on repetition. No pushing, no force. Her leg trembled as she lifted it a few inches, held, then lowered it back to the mat.

Seven... eight.

Eric moved around the kitchen. The low clatter of a blender. He'd been at home more lately, tapering for the race. Shorter runs plus rest. The nervous energy came out sideways, ricocheting into Dee.

"Nine," Dee said under her breath. She rolled onto her side and reset.

Eric came into the living room with a green-and-pink smoothie. He leaned against the wall and sipped through a straw.

"Can I help?"

"No," Dee said, then stopped herself. "Actually, yes." She strapped a stretchy resistance band around the ball of her foot and lay on her back. "Lift my leg."

Eric put his drink on the table. Cool latex in his hand, he straddled above Dee. "Tell me what you want." The two laughed. "You know what I mean."

Dee held her leg perpendicular to the floor. "Just raise it gently. Imagine your own IT band was tight."

"What's an IT band?"

Dee started to chuckle, then stopped. His training ended so abruptly; he was still an amateur runner, no thanks to her. Before guilt could engulf her, she spoke.

"Lay down next to me. I'll show you."

Eric got to the ground and held his leg in the same hamstring stretch as his wife, though much less elegant, even if she was nursing an injury. He groaned as he tried to straighten his leg.

"Ahhh," he sighed, enjoying the release. "A newsletter came in from the race director. Lots of international runners attending. Including a few elites from Kenya."

"With a prize pot like that, it'll attract the best of the best. Maybe—"

She swallowed the rest of her sentence. She feared for his body and his heart. Not to mention the pain of losing. The old urge to retreat, to quit, tugged at her.

Eric's breath shallowed as he hit a tight spot. "Oh. The credit card bill came."

There it was. The reason he was running: money. Dee lowered her leg.

"I want to tell you something," she said.

Eric stilled mid-stretch. "Okay..."

Dee wiped her hands on her shorts. Her heart kicked. "I've been feeling... desire. Not all the time. But it's there."

His eyes softened, then flickered. "Desire for what?"

She kept going before she lost her nerve.

"Sex." The word hung like a tetherball waiting to be swatted. "I'm not offering anything. I just... I knew I shouldn't keep it to myself." The last part was rushed.

Eric cleared his throat to bide his time. "Thank you for telling me," he said finally.

That was it. No follow-up. No "Do you want me?" No reaching. The moment held peacefully. Dee exhaled. Eric let his own leg return to earth.

Chapter 52

"That actually helps. Not the stretch." He laughed. "That helped too. Just the... you know. Knowing."

She smiled. "Good."

The old pattern twitched: her instinct to over-explain, to manage his feelings. But she fought back and let those urges go. Her skin hummed with pride and swelled with energy. Eric pushed himself from the floor and returned to his smoothie. Dee watched him walk lighter, easier. He was proud of himself too.

53

———

Training was finally behind them; the Blue Mountain Ultra had arrived. To avoid driving to the start line before dawn, they splurged on a cheap motel as close to the course as they could afford. Dee handed over her Visa for the eighty-dollar charge.

Either this adds to our debt, or it all disappears today.

Eric carried his own loop of dread.

What if I don't come in first? What if I get hurt? What if I let her down?

Instead of voicing it, he lifted his eyes toward the stained motel ceiling and prayed.

"I surrender this race, my doubts, and the outcome. Just don't let me get hurt. And please don't let us lose more money."

He tried to smile. Dee couldn't. They'd already spent hundreds on race fees, shoes, and gear. She was stressed from over-planning and a lack of help. Dee was Eric's one-woman pit crew. She mapped her stations carefully, favoring places where momentum mattered. She laid out bags with precision. Loosened laces. Portioned food. She knew how small mistakes turned into injuries. Eric was there to win without hiccups brought on by her.

They went to bed early. Eric slept. Dee didn't. She stared at the

164

popcorn ceiling, arms numb, afraid the power would cut out. Afraid of everything that happened when you let your guard down. By the time the alarm went off at 4 a.m., she was already exhausted.

Rain fell as they drove toward the start. Gray clouds sagged low over the mountains. It hung above them and next to them. Dee's limp an ominous reminder of running in rain.

Before they parted, Dee took Eric's hands and bowed her head. "Thank You for getting him here. Keep him strong. Keep him safe. He's done the work."

She dropped Eric as close to the start line as security would let her. Despite the weather, the energy was electric. Runners in ponchos stretched and did warm-up drills. A crowd of svelte teenagers surged by her. A swath of tutu-wearing middle-aged ladies clucked on through. Empty gel packs sucked clean along with discarded banana peels cluttered the pavement. Dee felt the buzz of the race vibrate through her sneakers. She wished she could run too.

Dee took Eric's bib number — 1818 — as a sign. Eights were good luck. Double numbers even better. But the downpour worsened, roads slicked, shoes soaked, and blisters bloomed. A different kind of luck entirely.

At mile fifteen, Dee unpacked her first station and noticed how much better prepared everyone else looked. Chairs. Umbrellas. Multiple people moving in sync.

I should've asked for help.

Running looked solitary, but it wasn't. That's why she'd built Run Café. That was why she'd wanted community yet somehow ended up alone. Her watch chimed. Eric's heart rate spiked as he hit a hill.

"He's climbing," she said aloud to herself. "It'll settle."

And it did. Back down to 120.

Elite runners crested the incline and flew past without stopping. A cluster of Kenyans tackled the hill together but separate, lean and fast. Their sneakers squeaked and squished in ever-growing puddles. They were gone in a flash. A bright flicker of pride swelled inside Dee.

It's nice to see some Black faces.

Eric appeared moments later. Hair plastered to his face, breathing controlled, eyes clear.

"What do you need?" she asked.

"A headband."

Of course, the one thing she forgot. Dee pulled off her snapback and handed it to him. He smiled, grateful.

"See you at thirty."

As he disappeared downhill, rain soaked through her shirt. Her curls frizzed and lifted. She saw her reflection in a car window and winced.

You look crazy.

Before she drove to the next station, she searched the car twice and came up empty. No hat. Then she remembered. She reached into her overnight bag and pulled out her sleeping bonnet, soft and warm. She slipped it over her damp hair.

You look nuts.

"I don't care what anyone thinks," she said aloud. Unapologetically Black.

By mile thirty, the rain turned relentless. The air was muggy and thick with wet pine and muddy earth. Dee set up her station with Vaseline and dry socks. A group of wet watchers in slickers cheered at passing runners. The pavement was soggy with abandoned sweatshirts, jogging pants, and even a lost shoe.

Eric appeared at the mile marker. His clothes soaked through with rain. Eyes red, lips chapped. Dee's own pupils dilated as she clocked him.

He's not sweating.

Not the healthy sheen she expected. Not the salt-stung shine she knew from training. His skin looked almost dry beneath the rain. A Black runner streaked past. Dee's mind worked fast.

If he were Black, he'd— She cut herself off. *If he were Black, he wouldn't be Eric.*

She studied her husband's cadence. Slightly quick and too eager. An ultramarathon demanded patience. *Slow down*, she wanted to tell him. The words pressed hard against her teeth. Voicing them would sound like fear, like doubt. Instead, she lifted the bottle of Gatorade.

"Drink this."

He took it and drank, then wiped his mouth with the back of his hand.

"You okay?" he asked as he changed his socks.

"I'm good. How are you?"

"I got this."

He was pushing himself too hard already. Before she could say anything, he disappeared into the pack. Dee checked her watch. His heart rate steady at 135.

He's fine, the numbers said.

Still, Dee worried. She stood there longer than she meant to, rain tapping her bonnet. Some people stared the way they gawked at mixed couples in Greenup. She watched the slower entrants pass by like they had all the time in the world.

54

Between mile thirty and mile forty-five, access to the race became dense with traffic. Dee drove access roads with her window cracked. Rain misted her face. Phone mounted to the dash, Eric's dot moved steadily across the screen. His numbers behaved, his pace stayed consistent, his heart rate high but not alarming.

He's trained for this. This is where it's supposed to hurt. The numbers don't lie.

Still, her mind kept returning to mile thirty. Dry skin. Overeagerness on the climb. The word *race* looped through her head in ways she didn't like. Not just the ultra — everything else layered inside of it. She rolled up her window and parked.

Around her, crews were already set up like small armies. Pop-up tents, folding chairs, dry bags stacked neatly. She laid out what she had anyway. Packets of gel, electrolytes, salt. A towel, already damp. She checked her phone. Eric's dot crept closer.

This is where it all evens out.

Runners came through in waves. Faces slack. Eyes glassy. Shoes caked with mud or trailing toilet paper. A man with blood soaking through his racer tank grimaced at every step. Dee scanned for Eric, refusing to put his face on those who were struggling.

"You're late," she said when he appeared. "I mean, you're here."

His hands shook as he reached for the bottle. He dropped the cap and groaned when he bent over to pick it up.

"Leave it," she said.

He did and resumed drinking. Orange liquid spilled down his chin, staining his bib.

"How do you feel?"

"Dunno. Fine?"

"You're doing great. Only seventeen miles to go. A little more than a half-marathon."

Eric shook his head. "Doesn't help."

"This is our last pit stop. How are your nipples?"

Eric's eyebrows knit across his forehead. "Okay. How are yours?"

Finally, laughter.

You could slow him now, a voice said. *Just a little.*

"You're still in it," she said instead. "You're right where you need to be."

He turned away. Jokes were over.

"Shoes?" she asked. "Gels? What do you want to carry?"

A shake of his head. She pressed a gel in his hand anyway. He took it without looking.

"You can do this," she said, feeling the lie register in her body before it left her mouth. She wanted to grab his shoulders. Wanted to say *this isn't worth your heart. I need you alive.*

Instead, she checked her watch and smiled.

"Go," she said. "I'll see you at the finish."

He left without a word.

Dee walked the gear back to her car. A Black family wearing matching shirts poured out of a minivan. She hated the way her mind kept reverting to the wrong race.

Focus on one thing at a time.

By the time she got to the finish line, roads were closed. Volunteers waved her Hyundai south, away from the action. She circled, recalculated, circled again. The crowd thickened. Her phone buzzed. Eric was three miles from the end.

Everything I could do is done.

She hated the relief that came with the thought.

Dee limped her way through the crowd. The race no longer belonged to the runners.

A marching band hammered out the *Rocky* theme. Spectators held drinks to offer runners. Gatorade, beer, Bloody Marys, anything liquid.

Rain fell, but no one cared. This was a revival. The Blue Mountain Ultra now a street party. The smell of sweat, rain, and booze comingled in the air.

Dee tried but couldn't get close. She was trapped behind bodies, four rows deep. Eric's dot pulsed closer and closer to the finish.

He's flying.

She started pushing. Apologies spilled out as she squeezed through tight gaps. She ducked elbows, slipped past strollers, navigated folding chairs taking up way too much space. Her Black skin helped White folks make room for her to pass through.

"Sorry... excuse me."

She reached the barricade and locked both hands around the cold metal, immoveable. Her phone vibrated. Mile 61.4.

"They're coming!" someone yelled.

Three runners crested the final hill together, legs churning. Two Black faces and one White man. Dee spotted Eric instantly. Mud-streaked, jaw clenched, eyes wild. Pride, rivalry, and prayer all tangled together before she could sort them out. She raised a fist high in the air. "GO, ERIC, GO!"

Eric surged. For a moment, he looked unstoppable. Then the light above shifted onto his face. Rain clung to his lashes. Sweat flooded his eyes. He squinted, faltered.

He can't see!

The two runners beside him pulled down their sunglasses and broke away. Arms pumping. Feet slapping hard against the pavement. The crowd surged forward. Bodies pressed in. Cheers, then screams.

Someone yelled, "MEDIC!"

Dee lost sight of Eric.

"Eric?!" Her voice vanished into the noise.

She pushed against the barricade. Heart slamming, eyes scanning bodies beyond the line. Out of nowhere, EMTs. A stretcher.

For the first time all day, Dee didn't know if Eric was alive.

55

By the last mile, Eric's legs stopped feeling like legs. Instead, they were Roman columns: heavy, unresponsive, and hardened every time his foot hit the pavement. His calves burned. His ears throbbed. His hips ached. His lungs were crystallized, like he couldn't take in enough air.

Sound pressed in from every direction. Cheering. Shouting. Cowbells. Music. Breath. It was a roar that vibrated through him. The smell was borderline unbearable: sweat, mud, something sharp and metallic he couldn't quite place.

That's blood.

He sucked back down a lump of vomit.

Focus, he told himself. *One more mile.*

Two runners were ahead of him, their strides long and elastic. He tried to match but let them determine the pace.

Not yet, he thought. *Not yet.*

His vision narrowed. The edges of the road blurred with rain. His eyes stung. He wiped his face with the back of his hand, making everything wetter.

Don't lose them.

He followed, tracking taut Black limbs.

For Dee, he thought. *Do it for Dee.*

Chapter 55

He surged. People cheered. Someone said, "Go 1818!" He vaguely remembered his bib.

My address?

Eric gained on the runners.

Third place takes home three thousand dollars. Not enough.

He imagined Dee at the barricade, willing him forward. His body obeyed, arms pumping, legs breaking free. The finish sign in front of him. The blast of a foghorn.

Did someone yell my name?

A sudden burst of sun cut through the clouds. The road flared bright, hot white.

I can't see!

He squinted and slowed. Two runners lowered sunglasses from the tops of their heads, then they were gone. The crowd cheered. Another flash of legs blew past him. The moment Eric's foot hit past the line, his body folded. Someone held him up. Another hand pressed against his chest. The noise dropped out, replaced by the sound of a rushing river between his ears.

"Sit him down!"

"Get him water!"

He tried to speak, but his mouth wouldn't let him. His heart slammed wildly. Fast and irregular. The butterfly was mad.

"MEDIC!" someone yelled too urgently.

Beep beep beep.

Cold hands, then heat. A strap tightening around his arm. A pulse pounded in his neck that didn't match the count being called out loud. He tried to lift his head. The world tilted. A face hovered over him, concerned, professional, not Dee.

"Easy," they said. "You're gonna be okay."

He was lowered onto a stretcher. The sky slid sideways, as gray and dirty as his shoes. He caught a glimpse of the crowd. Faces stretched and blurred. A mask pressed against his face. The cool rush of oxygen made him dizzy.

"Breathe."

His heart slowed. His eyelids closed.

"ERIC?!"

By the time he found Dee again, they were in the car. She drove without speaking, hands steady on the wheel, eyes fixed forward. He didn't look at her. If he did, he'd break. He didn't just lose a race; he'd failed at helping his wife and saving their marriage. He'd missed third place by milliseconds. Four seconds would have changed everything. It would give them breathing room. Fourth place meant nothing but a medal he'd already threw away.

At home, she drew him a bath and added ice to it. He watched her move with efficiency. He hated being doted on. Hated that he needed it. The tub burned like needles. He lowered himself slowly, breath shuddering as cold climbed his legs, his hips, his back. When he submerged, he counted the seconds.

One. Two. Three. Fourth place.

He came up gasping.

"That's cold," he sputtered. It was easier than saying anything else.

Dee sat on the edge of the tub, looking tired.

She thinks this is her fault. She thinks everything is her fault.

"It's not your fault," he told her. He could tell she didn't believe him.

When he got out, his body shook violently. He reached for a towel. She handed it to him without looking. He was small and shriveled. He thought of those plastic penises Dee tucked away in secret. The littlest one at the forefront of his mind.

"Sorry," he muttered.

"You have nothing to be sorry for." She rested her arms on his shoulders.

"I'm sorry I lost."

"No apologies." She lifted his chin. "We'll figure it out. We always do."

The towel slipped to the ground. He stood naked in front of her. She stayed fully dressed. It mirrored everything between them. His openness, her armor.

"I'm sorry," she said then. "For everything."

He pulled her into a hug without thinking. Her body fit into his like memory. Desire surged and poked her. She stepped back.

"Hey," she said, gently, with a smile.

"Sorry. I can't help biology."

He saw conflict cross her face, then a smile. He loved her for not making him feel worse.

"When you're ready, I want to show you something," she said.

"What?"

"A video."

He blinked. "A video?"

"A porn. The one I was watching when you came in."

The memory landed between them. Heavy, honest, and terrifying.

"Why?"

"Homework."

Eric thought of the race, of surrendering control, of learning a new sport late in life — and Dee learning her body.

"Okay," he said, meaning it.

Dee wanted to fix everything but couldn't. This was a start.

56

Dee and Eric spent the rest of the day in bed. Creams, lotions, lube, the wand, and dilators scattered across sheets, floor, and skin. The laptop lay on the ground, closed.

Eric fell asleep immediately afterward. He always did. Ten minutes or an hour — it didn't matter. His body shut down completely, as if he emptied out everything at once. He spent himself everywhere. Today, it felt earned.

Dee watched his chest rise and fall. When he woke and found her still there, naked beside him, he reached for her without hesitation. No apology, no doubt, just love.

After their third time that weekend, Dee welcomed the pause. She lay on her back and stared out the window at the lake, its surface darkening as clouds rolled in again. Another storm was coming. Even inside, she felt the temperature drop. She didn't leave the house anymore. Fear kept her a hermit. Today, something moved her to break free.

She rolled carefully off the mattress, grateful for its silence. Eric slept on, mouth open, breath soft and unguarded. She slipped into her terrycloth robe, pulled on her old rabbit slippers, padded through the kitchen, and eased out the back door. The cold air slapped her awake.

Chapter 56

She smoothed her hair, but the act was futile. It didn't matter. Eric wanted her exactly as she was — heavier, guarded, broke, and healing. Seeing herself through his eyes softened something she'd been gripping for years. She stepped farther into the yard. Their yard.

I built this place, she thought. *Not with lumber the way my dad used to, but with hope, grief, and stubbornness.*

Eric added onto it: onto the house and onto her life. Together, they'd made something solid and barely lived in it. They never walked the land, never gardened or pruned or sat in the three-seasons room together. That room became storage. The property did too.

You took this place for granted.

The thought landed. "Help me," she whispered.

The answer came without explanation.

Let go.

The words hit her the way gravity does when you realize you're already falling.

"You want me to give up my house?"

Again: *let go.*

This place that held her after her family died. The only constant she'd known. She'd lived here longer than anywhere else. Even Peoria.

"I don't know where I'd go. I don't know who I am without this."

Wind cut through her robe, sharp and insistent. The voice was audible now.

Let go.

Dee stood, heart pounding, as the idea cracked open — unfinished, ungentle, unavoidable. This time, she didn't try to argue back.

57

She came inside and stood in the dark kitchen. The warm air surrounded her. Eric's breath steady and deep from the bedroom. She let him stay sleeping and sat at the table to pray.

Let go.

The words hung like fruit flies she felt guilty for swatting and even worse for ignoring. She knew what to do. She'd been given an answer. But knowing and doing sat on opposite sides of something she couldn't quite cross.

Dee didn't know why her stomach tightened when she thought about talking to Eric about the voice. They'd already survived worse.

But sounding crazy?

That was part of the problem. She never told anyone how God spoke to her — not out loud, not in visions, not as something unmistakable and internal. His voice was solid yet ethereal. It was always with her, quiet and unavoidable. Talking about it made her embarrassed. Another shame pushed away.

"I'm afraid of rejection," Dee once admitted to Dr. Ryerson.

"Rejection isn't the framework. Communication is."

Dee understood the words. She just didn't live them. After the backyard — after *let go* — Dee knew avoidance was no longer an option. A half hour later, her talk with God ended. He told her what to do. The rest was up to her.

Eric was awake reading a library book about running he never once touched before the race. Now he couldn't stop thinking about what came next. Another ultra. Another goal. Another prize pot waiting to be claimed.

"We need to talk," Dee said.

Eric looked up. "Uh oh."

She sat beside him. No easing in. "Remember when you came home angry? When you thought I was manipulating your runs?"

His shoulders tightened. "Yeah."

"You were right."

He blinked. "About what?"

"I monitored your heart rate with sex."

"What? Why?"

"I was trying to strengthen your heart. That's why we were doing it so often."

Color drained from his face. "You didn't want to? You didn't enjoy it?"

"Not at first."

"Dee—" Eric got off the bed they'd just made plenty of love in. "Why would you do that? If you didn't want to, why didn't you just say no?"

"I was afraid." She looked at her hands. "I was worried. I didn't know how else to get you ready in time."

"That doesn't make it okay."

"I know."

"You used me. You *lied* to me. Do you know how that feels?"

"I do now."

Eric went into the bathroom. Dee followed, keeping her distance.

"You shared something intimate with me," he said, splashing water on his face, "and I didn't even know what was happening. I thought we were connecting. I thought you wanted me."

"I'm sorry. I know it was wrong."

He stared at himself in the mirror, avoiding her gaze behind him. He couldn't look.

"That might be the worst part. That you weren't really there."

"I was willing, though," Dee said, choosing her words carefully. "I trained my body. I wanted it to work."

"When did you start *liking* it?"

She hesitated. "The day I got hurt."

"That long?" He turned sharply.

"That was my first orgasm."

Eric's face dropped. "You never told me that."

"I didn't know how."

He shook his head, overwhelmed. "Please leave."

"Eric—"

"I need to be alone, Dee."

She stepped back as he closed the bathroom door on her. She stood in the bedroom, heart pounding. Everything she feared was happening. She sat on the bed, facing the door. There was still more and she couldn't stop now.

"I know I haven't been honest," she said through the wood. "I don't want secrets anymore."

No response.

"I didn't understand intimacy or consent before. That's not an excuse. It's the truth."

Still nothing.

"There's something else," she said, voice shaking. "Something important."

"Seriously? What now?"

"God told me to let the house go." The words came out fast. "To sell it."

"*Told* you?" Eric's voice sounded mocking.

"He spoke to me. Here." Dee pointed at her heart as if Eric could see it. "I know it sounds stupid, but it's true."

He didn't respond.

"Eric?"

She stood and reached for the doorknob. The door opened

before she touched it. Eric's eyes were red and his face unreadable. Dee turned away and lay on the bed, bracing.

This is what rejection feels like, she thought. *This is what I was afraid of. I deserve this.*

The bed dipped as Eric sat beside her. She felt his hand rest on her back. He didn't speak, but he was there.

58

Eric sat on the edge of the bed long after Dee stopped talking. He could feel her beneath his palm — warm, shaking. The room smelled like sweat, soap, sex, and the faint, clean chill of Kentucky rain. Everything was exposed. Not just his body but his memories. He replayed her words, not the way she said them, but the meaning behind them.

She didn't want to have sex with me. She faked it all.

It lodged in him like a stone covered in thorns. He'd spent his life afraid of being unwanted. His father had carved that fear early. It didn't matter how many times Dee reached for him, how many times she touched him, moaned, or pulled him close. The revelation rewired the past.

She'd been somewhere else the whole time.

He paced the bathroom, bare feet cold against the floor. He felt different, lonely. He didn't know what to do with Dee's truth that she'd wanted him *eventually*. That her body learned him, even if her heart lagged behind. That wasn't assault. But it wasn't love either. And then there was the other thing.

God told me to sell the house.

Eric pressed his palms into his eyes. He believed in God. That wasn't the problem. Dee's God felt different — urgent and demanding. Loud in a way Eric didn't recognize. What scared him wasn't what she heard. It was that everything required destruction.

Sell the house. Burn it down and call it faith.

He sat beside her. Dee lay face-down. Shoulders trembling. Smaller than she usually was. Stripped of defenses. He knew what manipulation looked like. This wasn't it. He thought about the race. How he'd run himself into the ground for them. How he'd wanted to fix things with his body because he didn't know how else to help. He didn't resent her for that. Not really. He felt proud, chosen. But now even that felt shaky.

Have I been useful or just plain used?

The thought made his heart ache. He placed his hand on her back because it was the only thing he knew how to do that didn't make things worse. He didn't forgive her yet. He couldn't. But he also couldn't walk away. That scared him most of all.

"I don't know what to do with this," he said finally.

Beneath his hand, Dee's breath trembled.

"I believe you," he continued. "About trying. About wanting sex later. About being scared."

She didn't turn over. Just exhaled.

"But I need time. I need space to understand what's mine in all this. And what isn't."

She sighed into the mattress.

"And moving," he added. "That's not something I can hear yet. Not like this."

Her breath audibly expanded.

"But I do know one thing. I don't want secrets either." His hand stayed where it was. "I don't know if forgiveness comes first or understanding. Or even anger. But I don't think this is the end. At least not tonight."

Dee turned her head just enough for him to see her eyes. Red, wet, and searching. He didn't pull away. He didn't pull her closer either. He stayed, and that was enough.

59

Eric carried another box from the house toward the U-Haul, arms locked tight around its weight. Dee sat on the open tailgate with a Sharpie in one hand and a clipboard in the other. Inside the truck sat lamps, tables, and stacks of boxes filling the space all the way to the ceiling.

"This is the last of them," Eric said, wiping his forehead with the back of his wrist. "All the books."

She labeled the box "books."

"All the heavy stuff's done." Eric drained the rest of his water bottle. Sweat soaked his headband and darkened the collar of his T-shirt. He didn't seem bothered.

Dee watched him drink. The way his arms flexed as he crushed the empty bottle and slid it into his pocket. They didn't talk much while packing. They didn't need to. Something between them had changed. They touched differently now. Less urgency, more attention. Sex wasn't frequent, but it was honest. Therapy was helping Dee find her words. Gentle. Soft. Harder. She could tell Eric what she wanted without him asking. When she didn't want anything, she said that too. There was no training, no agenda. She — they — were starting anew.

Eric glanced at her clipboard. "What's next?"

Chapter 59

She shook her head. "A photo break."

He walked toward the end of the drive where the SOLD sign stood crooked in the dirt. The house had gone fast. Four offers the first day the listing went live. A bidding war by the weekend. The final number erased their debt and then some. Enough to breathe. When the realtor called, Dee laughed then went still at the reality she would be leaving her second home almost as abruptly as she left her first. Only this time, she was not running away.

Eric stood beside the sign, hands on his hips, surveying the land like it finally belonged to him. A few months ago, this driveway felt like a trap. The house was unwelcoming. Every room held his failure. Now it was neutral. A place they both lived.

Eric turned back toward her. "Here?"

She raised her phone. "Yeah. Right there."

He smiled a genuine grin. Dee took the photo.

Later, when the truck was packed and the keys sat on the counter where strangers would soon find them, they stood in the empty living room and didn't rush to fill the silence. That night, they slept on an air mattress in the center of the floor. The house echoed around them. Eric lay on his back, staring at the ceiling. Dee turned toward him.

"Does this feel weird to you?" she asked.

He thought for a moment. "Yeah."

"Bad weird?"

"No," he said. "Just... different."

They didn't talk about forgiveness or homework or what any of it meant. Eric reached for her hand instead. Dee let him. They stayed like that until sleep came.

In the morning, sunlight filled the bare room. Dee stood first. She padded into the kitchen, brewed the last of the coffee, and drank it standing at the counter. When Eric joined her, he leaned against the sink, shoulder brushing hers. She didn't move away.

Neither of them mentioned what still hurt. Neither of them said the word *sorry*. But when they finished up their packing, Eric was there for her and Dee noticed.

60

———————

Eric woke before the sun. The house was quiet in a way that felt final. No hum of appliances, just the soft click of cooling walls and the distant sound of Dee moving somewhere down the hall.

He lay on the air mattress, feeling a dull ache everywhere at once. Not the sharp stiffness that came after his race. This was deeper. A soreness that came from holding onto something too tightly without setting it down.

He replayed Dee's words, the ones she'd said in the bedroom. The ones through the bathroom door. The ones that landed hardest because they were honest, not careful. The conversation still churned his stomach. He wasn't angry the way he'd expected to be. Rage would have been easier. It would have given him something clean to push against. What he felt instead was grief that sat on him like an elephant and refused to move.

He wanted her. That was the worst part. He wanted her every time. Wanted her even when she was distant, even when she turned away, even when she stayed silent beside him. Desire was never the issue for him. It still wasn't. What hurt was learning that wanting didn't mean being wanted back, a feeling that was new and old at the same time.

Eric rolled onto his side and stared at the far wall. He thought about his mother. About what she'd once told him years after his father left.

The worst betrayal isn't the cheating. It's realizing you were alone while you thought you were loved.

He didn't think Dee meant to hurt him. Her words came out before his heart could catch up. But if he forgave her, he had to risk being hurt again.

The empty house creaked. Dee's footsteps paused near the air mattress, then moved on. She was giving him space.

Eric sat up slowly and ground himself, feet to the floor. His body protested, but he welcomed the sensation. Pain meant something real happened. He walked into the bathroom and poured a glass of water. His hands shook, not from weakness, but from restraint. There were a hundred things he could say to her: accusations, questions, scriptures. None would move them forward. He wanted to be a man who stayed because he chose to.

When he came into the kitchen, he stopped short. Dee opened a box marked KITCHEN. His usual mug sat on the counter, full and steamy. Her eyes flicked to his face, searching for signs of anger or judgment, but he gave her none of them.

"I made coffee," she said.

"Thanks." He picked up his mug.

They stood there, the space between them thick, but not hostile.

"I don't expect you to forgive me," Dee said. "I just need you to know the truth."

"I'm not okay with what happened." His voice surprised him with its steadiness.

Dee's hands wrapped tighter around her mug.

"And I don't think we pretend it didn't hurt. But I'm not going to punish you forever."

Her breath swelled.

"I can't promise I won't need time," he said. "Or that I won't feel it again later. But I don't want to live in resentment. And I don't want to leave."

Dee looked down at her hands. "I don't deserve that."

"Maybe not. But I'm not doing this because you deserve it. I'm doing it because I don't want bitterness to decide my life."

She was listening. Eric reached for her. She didn't pull away. Outside, a truck passed. Somewhere in the house, something shifted and settled. Eric squeezed her hand once, then let go.

"I'm going to load the rest of the stuff," he said.

Dee watched him move past her, toward the door, toward the work that still needed doing. She would meet him there and take it one step at a time.

61

The office smelled like coffee and old books. Dee sat across from Pastor Marlena with her hands folded so tightly the color in her fingertips drained.

"So," Marlena said gently. "Tell me what you're afraid of."

Dee didn't look up. "That I'm a bad person." With no response from Marlena, she continued. "I didn't lie about loving him or wanting to stay married. I just didn't want sex. I trained myself into wanting it through masturbation, porn, and maybe a little force." She glanced up at Marlena. "I don't know what that makes me."

Marlena leaned back, giving the words room. "Did Eric force you?" she asked.

"No."

"Did he pressure you?"

"No."

"Did you feel free to say no?"

Dee's throat tightened. "I don't know if I knew I could."

"That matters."

Dee's voice shook. "People say if you don't want it, it's rape. I didn't want it. Not at first. So, was it rape?"

Marlena held her gaze. "Consent isn't a single moment. It's

alive. It changes. What makes sex harmful isn't that desire grows or shifts, it's when someone feels they can't speak honestly about where their desire actually is."

"My body had to catch up to my marriage."

"That's purity culture talking." Now it was Dee's turn to lean in. "It teaches women their bodies are late to their lives. What you did wasn't evil. And it wasn't rape. It was disconnected. You left yourself out of the room. And when people do that long enough, they start using their bodies like tools."

"So, I hurt him," Dee said, jaw tightening.

"Yes, and you hurt yourself. You're not being punished. You're being asked to stay present. To notice when your body says yes. To stop when it says no."

Tears slipped down Dee's face. "I thought God wanted obedience," she whispered.

Marlena smiled softly. "He wants your love and trust. That doesn't come from sex."

"What if I don't always know what I want?"

"Then you tell the truth about that. That's consent too."

For the first time, Dee understood what it meant to submit.

62

Eric and Dee stood beside a vibrant tree at the top of Bruce's Peak in Elmira, Ontario. Its leaves were already turning, the explosion of color loud against the gray sky.

"It's a yellow poplar," Dee said in awe.

"Yeah," Eric said. "Mom's ashes were sprinkled here. She loved walking up this hill, so I thought this would be a good place for her to keep roaming."

Dee took his hand. "It's beautiful."

They'd come to Elmira for Dee to see where Eric grew up and finally meet his parents. Joanne's resting place was their first stop. The tree overlooked the town the same way his mother once had. Eric spread a blanket on the grass, smoothing it longer than necessary. They unpacked food from Bonnie Lou's Café, the Mennonite restaurant his mother used to frequent. Egg salad, pickles, pie wrapped in wax paper. The air smelled like damp leaves and warm bread.

He looked out over Elmira. A familiar tug pulled at him. He missed the simplicity of Canadian life. The way time moved slowly and memories were cemented by the weather. Eric took his wife's hand and squeezed it. She squeezed back.

They ate slowly. Neither of them spoke much. Eric watched

clouds drift across the sky, as slow-moving as his thoughts. Dee watched him. The way his leg bounced, then stilled. The way he kept clearing his throat as if rehearsing words he wasn't ready to say.

After lunch, Dee gave him space. She carried the empty containers to a nearby trash bin and sat on a bench a short distance away. Close enough to see. Far enough to let him be alone.

Eric stood near the tree, hands jammed in pockets. For a long moment, he kept quiet, staring at the ground beneath it, the place where his mother no longer was. The silence stretched, his heart racing as he tried to breathe through pain.

"I hope you've met the Morelands up there. Maybe you've seen Dad too." His voice broke before he could finish.

He wiped at his face with the heel of his palm, embarrassed by how quickly the tears came. He stayed a few more minutes, saying things Dee couldn't hear. Things he'd never said out loud before. The word "forgive" among the many.

On their way down, they passed a small cemetery. Howard Taylor's headstone sat near the gate. His initials carved at the top. Beneath them, a small cross. Dee stopped to look. Eric's body went rigid, like he'd hit an invisible wall. His hands grew clammy.

"There. You've seen it. Let's go."

Dee clung tighter. "He'd want to see you." She led Eric inside the ivy-covered gate.

They stood in front of his father's grave. Eric looked everywhere but at the stone. He couldn't without crying. His eyes lifted to the sky. To the gate. To Dee. Finally, he looked to the gravesite, then clung to Dee and sobbed.

"I'm sorry, Dad. I didn't mean it when I said I hated you. I hope you can forgive me."

Dee held her husband, feeling the weight of his grief as his words settled. A blue jay landed nearby. She couldn't help but smile. The bird chirped its welcome, then disappeared up the hill like it was taking the good news back to Joanne.

63

Dee had put this day off for twenty-five years. All morning, she stood in their walk-in closet, cycling through a small handful of dresses to find which one fit and which one felt right. The closet itself still felt unfamiliar. Much smaller than the one in Kentucky. But it held what they needed — and what she actually wore.

Outside the window, Peoria moved soundlessly. Snow clung to sidewalk edges. Bare branches lined Adams Street. A city accepting winter without apologizing for it.

Eric passed behind her, already dressed. He wore a tailored suit he'd bought secondhand — vintage Italian wool, soft at the elbows, pressed, and clean. It fit like it was meant for him. Since recouping their losses, thrifting became a skill and second nature to them both.

Eric accepted a position as assistant hockey coach at Bradley University. He left the house before sunrise most days, returning with the smell of cold air and rink sweat still clinging. He still ran, though much shorter distances, with no watch screaming metrics. Sometimes he was alone. Sometimes with Dee. Sometimes not at all. It was the sometimes that made the difference.

Dee still searched for her professional footing. She worked part-time at a local running shop on Main. Fitting shoes, giving gait advice. The owner encouraged her to bring in baked goods on Saturdays. She became good at baking. A new skill Eric loved.

Some runners lingered after their purchases, talking races, injuries, life. It wasn't Run Café, but it wasn't nothing either. Her business and passion lived in her the way a favorite song does. Faint, unmistakable, looping with love.

"Just pick something." She pulled off a dress she'd already tried on.

"What'd you say, sweetheart?" Eric called from the kitchen.

"I'm talking to myself," she called back, adjusting her new eyeglasses.

Weeks ago, when Dee finally walked through the grand doors of her childhood church, Pastor Wilcox crossed the room immediately. He was older than she remembered, slower in his step, but his genuine smile was the same.

"Dee Moreland," he said, pulling her into an embrace. "How I've missed you."

She wept, sobs thick with guilt. "I should've been there—"

"Hush, DeeDee. I would've left too."

Her life changed so suddenly and also not changed at all.

In the closet, indecision pressed her. The dress she'd settled on looked too sad. She sat on the edge of the bed, head in hands. Eric appeared in the doorway holding a gift-wrapped box.

"I figured today might come with decision fatigue," he said.

She choked back a laugh and it came out a snort. It was all she had in her. He handed her the box. Inside, a kitenge dress bloomed in her hands — orange, green, black. Celebration fabric. Ancestral cloth. Clothes to welcome her home.

"Eric," she whimpered.

"It seemed right for the occasion."

How right he was.

The two drove in silence, snow ticking softly beneath their tires. At the cemetery, the air was brittle and bright. Dee carried lilies. Eric held two bouquets of white roses. Their breath ebbed and flowed between them like punctuation. At her family's head-stones, Dee let tears flow.

"Hi, Mama." She sniffed as she placed the lilies gently, as if setting a child to sleep. "Hi, Daddy. Hi, Sister."

Beside her, Eric laid his roses on the two headstones, tears streaking his face too.

"Mom, Dad, Rashida — this is Eric. Thank you for sending him to me."

She stood longer than she thought she could without collapsing into a crying heap. Grief and gratitude braided together, keeping her upright.

They didn't leave immediately. They walked the perimeter of the cemetery, reading names, guessing stories. Dee was tired but surprisingly not shattered. She was doing hard, impossible things she never believed she'd be able to do.

On the drive home, they talked about dinner, stopped at the co-op, and bagged their groceries. Dee received compliments for her beautiful dress.

That night, in their small kitchen, Dee whisked a batter while Eric dried dishes. Their hips bumped, their hands touched. Eric kissed the back of Dee's neck and she let him. No need to reciprocate. Just enjoy.

Later, in bed, she reached for him.

"This is what I want," she said.

They moved slowly. No watches. No plans. No fear of what anything meant. Two bodies moving together. Not fused. Not separate. A marriage in sync.

Afterward, they slept tangled together in the quiet of their new life in Peoria. Their families weren't there, but Dee and Eric were.

And so was God.

ACKNOWLEDGMENTS

SUBMIT could not have been made without the support of the ladies from Mixed Race Book Club — my O.G. beta readers and friends for life — Kristina Sullivan, Emily Janes, and Stefanie Elkins.

Thank you to my cover designer Steve Kuhn, developmental editor Mark O'Brien, proofreader Robin Thompson, and photographer Ian Salmon for making me feel comfortable enough to add a picture of myself in at the back of this book. (It was going to be an illustration.)

Special thanks to Dr. Erica Oberman of the UCLA Menopause Clinic for keeping me healthy, Dr. Aerial Ellis of Black Women Pray for keeping me sane, Coach David A. Levine of the Los Angeles Road Runners for teaching me to run at my lactate threshold, and Jesi Rojas for helping me cross the LA Marathon finish line.

To Cara, Helen, Desireé, Tricia, Natalie, Nicole, and Rob, thank you for being my sisters and brother (some from another mother).

To my parents, thank you for always supporting my dreams.

To my husband, thank you for your patience, understanding, and endless forgiveness.

Last but always first, God. I write about surrender to practice it more. Thank You for Your gentle reminders to let it all go.

ABOUT THE AUTHOR

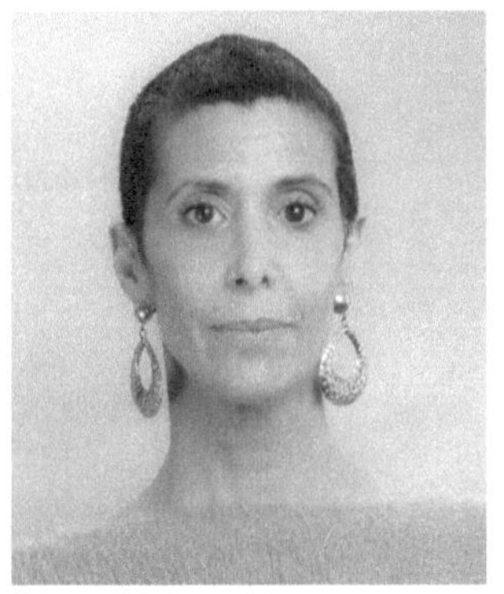

SUBMIT is Natasha Lewin's debut novel. She lives in Los Angeles with her husband and Simba, her dog. Learn more: natashalewin.com.